San Antonio Sci-Fi & Fantasy Authors Presents:

Tertiary LANDS

Short Stories of Sci-Fi & Fantasy
Volume I

Featuring Work By:
C.M. Bratton
Kevin Looney
Patrick Neal
JT Street
Michael Wigington

Edited by:
C. M. Bratton

Copyright © 2019.

ISBN: 9781692554538

All rights reserved.

This book is protected under the copyright laws of the United States of America.

Any reproduction or other unauthorized use of the material or artwork herein is prohibited.

This is a work of fiction. The character, incidents, and dialogues are products of the authors' imaginations and are not to be construed as real.

Cover art by ROBOT9000/Luis A Ruiz.

TABLE OF CONTENTS

Dedication ----------------------------------- 4
Acknowledgements --------------------------- 5
Note from the Editor ----------------------- 6
Quotes --------------------------------------- 7
The Silent Song ------------------------------ 8
A New Beginning ---------------------------- 11
The Secret of the Springs ------------------ 16
Tales from Applebottom ------------------- 35
The Sentinel --------------------------------- 43
Refuge of the Remnant --------------------- 53
Incident at Kramer Ridge ------------------ 61
Number Fourteen --------------------------- 78
Behind These Eyes ------------------------- 87
About SASFA -------------------------------- 96
About the Authors -------------------------- 97

ACKNOWLEDGEMENTS

No book is possible without the help of many people.

First and foremost, many thanks to the fans of our first group effort, Secondary Worlds, which won 1st Place in Speculative Poetry for the Texas Association of Author Best Book Awards in 2019. Because of that, we're jumping into new territory here with Tertiary Lands — short stories ranging from deep space to the bottom of the seas.

Also thanks to all the members of SASFA for their continuing work in the sci-fi & fantasy genres — let's keep inspiring each other.

Thanks to all of the contributors to this book for their stories. Special thanks for copy editing each other's work and making sure everything works.

And finally, special thanks to our cover artist, Robot9000, for his whimsical yet intense artwork that perfectly captures the range of work within this book.

DEDICATION

Once more,
to all of those lovers of the
fantastical, mythological, legendary,
fabled, imagined, boundary-crossing
worlds where our stories live.

Don't stop believing.

NOTE FROM THE EDITOR

Back in 2017, I had the pleasure of attending World Fantasy Con as an author. I met some of my idols and many other authors who were as passionate as me about the sci-fi & fantasy genres.

It was there the idea for a poetry book was first born, and that book went on to win an award in 2019. I considered following that with a second volume to build on the first. And that's definitely still in the plan.

But at the same time, I was planning a book of short stories to add to my Borderlands books, and I found myself staring at my file of short stories that were just mostly sitting around.

I have written short stories for as long as I could write, but I've never done too much with them. As I reviewed prepping for a second volume of speculative poetry, my eyes kept drifting back to the file and thinking about short stories.

To that end, I sent out an email to the previous authors to get their thoughts, and they were all immediately on board. I also sent out a call of submissions on our SASFA FB page and heard back from more people than I expected. I set a date to turn stories in, and surprisingly, not very many people were ready. But enough were for me to begin piecing this book together and jump into editing these stories.

So again, here we are with our first volume of short stories set in the realm of the fantastical and almost possible. I hope you enjoy jumping into these stories and exploring new realms, dreamscape, and TERTIARY LANDS.   -C.M. Bratton

"We are an impossibility
in an impossible universe."

-Ray Bradbury

~*~

"Fantasy is a necessary
ingredient in living."

-Dr. Seuss

~*~

The Silent Song
C.M. Bratton

He embraced her.

The sight of it was lancing agony, a man-sized spear that snagged my viscera and ripped it asunder. A hole grew inside me, grief replacing the brief joy I'd known.

Perhaps that was why I found myself drowning, gasping for air, unable to see past the haze of pain obscuring my vision. My life had been an unending series of disappointment, longing, and loneliness, tempered only slightly by the music that poured out of me, ever waiting for my call.

I'd few friends, and fewer still who understood my need to escape the narrow confines of growing up the youngest of twelve sisters, all of us bound to obey my father's every dictate as he ruled the kingdom with an iron fist. I'd both loved and hated him, for I'd always felt twisted in nets under his relentless regard, trapped and buried and destined to live out my life without ever seeing the world.

So I'd escaped. And I'd come to know what happiness was.

But it was too short a time.

He embraced her.

Countless images swirled in and out of my mind, faster than I wanted to remember, too slow to forget. The waving fronds of a coral reef. The soft embrace of sand. The sharp rip of scales. The unexpected pressure in my chest. The fear. That first gulp of air. Crushing air, forcing me into the sand, unable to move or resist.

His voice. His hands. His arms curling around me, lifting my body, carrying me to his home. I'd met his gaze, not understanding that it wasn't wonder that lit his gaze, but lust as he stared at my naked, willing form.

I gave him everything he asked. Everything except my songs, because my voice was hidden even from me. Still, I hoped it would be enough. It had to be enough. He was my joy. I ignored the little aches in my body, the sharp pain of his first entry, too entranced with the feel of his skin against mine, the sharp stretch of legs... my legs.

Whenever I was alone, I stared at them, marveling, running my hands up and down their smooth, muscled lengths. Later, when his hands echoed my own, touching every part of me, I thought I might go mad from the joy inside me, from the need to share the song of my love that echoed in my mind.

But I'd made a bargain, and I regretted nothing. I was his, and I thought he was mine. My long-missed voice couldn't share the melody straining at the edges of my throat, but my hands could. My legs did, wrapping around him with all the strength granted to me by the sea.

He held me in return, and I wanted nothing more. We were a song together. The only one that mattered.

He embraced her.

My body contracted with pain, spasming there on the sandy beach, my legs stolen, trapped once more by a tail that denied me the wonders of the land. Sun sparkled against scales I'd once admired, the reflected light floating up into the breeze. Waves lashed against me where I remained wedged between rocks, forced to watch the betrayal of she who'd given me such hope. He embraced her, his eyes shadowed by her power, and even then, I wanted to save him.

But as he leaned down and pressed his lips against hers, my reason fled. Anguish took over, a sorrow that echoed through the water and deep below. Perhaps my father felt it. Perhaps he was moved by mercy. Perhaps, he knew as I did that it was too late to change anything.

As I wept, as I stretched out my arms and screamed futilely, my voice still silenced, a wave swept over me. As it receded, so did my grief.

I looked away from the sight of them, from the death of my dream, out to the sea which was wild and yet had always felt like a prison. I understood then that freedom was about choice.

"Yes," I mouthed.

I stretched out my arms, embracing it all. Water churned beneath me. Perhaps it hurt, the dissolution of my flesh, but it was swift. And what was the suffering of my body compared to the violation of my soul?

My body thinned, became translucent. Light streamed through me. The sound of their merriment faded. I uncoiled from my prison and became lighter, so light I no longer felt anything. I know longer *was*.

I embraced myself.

Then I was gone, and only sea foam remained to mark my passing.

A NEW BEGINNING
KEVIN LOONEY

Thirty years without a spoken word ends when the sun slams into my face to raise me from death. Five letters join together as something recognizable, almost tangible, spits out from my mouth like water from a drowning man.

"Light."

I don't even have time to process the miraculous event before a group of men dressed in white suits burst into my bedroom. I follow my first instinct. I run.

I hear one of the men hit the floor with a loud thud as I push through them and out the door. Living at the top of a ten-story apartment building no longer sounds like a good idea. The elevator is broken, which means I'm forced to descend one hundred and sixty steps. I go as fast as I can with the presence of my pursuers looming over me. I don't know why they're chasing me, but I have no desire to find out.

When I reach the bottom, I immediately dash for the street exit. I turn right without thought or reason. I trip over a crack in the sidewalk and nearly split my skull on the dirty pavement. My hands accept the brunt of the costly mistake, absorbing the shock of the impact as my already rough skin grinds against the tiny, concrete bumps. While I push myself back up, my eyes glimpse the splattered image of an unspoken word on the ground. It is red and could have been the color of my blood.

I have never said this curse aloud, but here it is, staring me down like a bull ready to skewer me. I don't understand what's happening, but there is no time to think. I must keep moving.

My worn tennis shoes resume their frenzied crusade to escape capture. I push my way through a small group of teenagers. They pause their ramblings of inconsequential nonsense as I roll forward like a barrel down a steep decline. I expect an endless salute of four-letter words to be expelled, but there is only Rene Descartes. Much like the esteemed philosopher, they discuss the mysteries of reality with the fervor of someone who believes he's stumbled upon a wholly original concept.

For a moment, I look back to see the words "I Am" floating above their heads like in a comic. Perhaps they believe themselves gods. Young people sometimes do. To me, they are just a distraction. After turning sharply down an alley, I pause to check on an old, homeless man who may be having a heart attack. It's difficult to assess the exact nature of his situation while I focus on my own plights.

I absorb a tankard of air into my lungs and realize for the first time that I should be unconscious from exhaustion. Somehow, I do not feel tired, hungry, or even thirsty. The only thing I crave is more words. More speech.

I can't control it. The words find voice when they want. I do not choose them.

"Water."

Not enough.

"Dirt."

The ground shakes for a moment, and I fear I will soon have unwanted company. I continue moving once I am confident the aged and disheveled man before me is not expiring. There is no time to linger in the hidden crevices of the city.

As I pass the man's shadow, I feel the darkness seize me. Images invade my mind. They are instances in time—pictures of hateful acts throughout history visualized like a diagram along the connectors within my brain.

I don't stop running, but I close my eyes and shake my head, willing myself free from this disease. I do this for several seconds and wonder why I haven't run into a wall. When I finally open my eyes, I'm no longer on the streets of the city, but in a garden. Only, it is unlike anything I've seen before. It's more like an unfinished sketch, a landscaper's blueprint.

"Orange."

More.

"Yellow."

More.

I gave him everything he asked. Everything except my songs, because my voice was hidden even from me. Still, I hoped it would be enough. It had to be enough. He was my joy. I ignored the little aches in my body, the sharp pain of his first entry, too entranced with the feel of his skin against mine, the sharp stretch of legs... my legs.

Whenever I was alone, I stared at them, marveling, running my hands up and down their smooth, muscled lengths. Later, when his hands echoed my own, touching every part of me, I thought I might go mad from the joy inside me, from the need to share the song of my love that echoed in my mind.

But I'd made a bargain, and I regretted nothing. I was his, and I thought he was mine. My long-missed voice couldn't share the melody straining at the edges of my throat, but my hands could. My legs did, wrapping around him with all the strength granted to me by the sea.

He held me in return, and I wanted nothing more. We were a song together. The only one that mattered.

He embraced her.

My body contracted with pain, spasming there on the sandy beach, my legs stolen, trapped once more by a tail that denied me the wonders of the land. Sun sparkled against scales I'd once admired, the reflected light floating up into the breeze. Waves lashed against me where I remained wedged between rocks, forced to watch the betrayal of she who'd given me such hope. He embraced her, his eyes shadowed by her power, and even then, I wanted to save him.

But as he leaned down and pressed his lips against hers, my reason fled. Anguish took over, a sorrow that echoed through the water and deep below. Perhaps my father felt it. Perhaps he was moved by mercy. Perhaps, he knew as I did that it was too late to change anything.

As I wept, as I stretched out my arms and screamed futilely, my voice still silenced, a wave swept over me. As it receded, so did my grief.

I looked away from the sight of them, from the death of my dream, out to the sea which was wild and yet had always felt like a prison. I understood then that freedom was about choice.

"Yes," I mouthed.

I stretched out my arms, embracing it all. Water churned beneath me. Perhaps it hurt, the dissolution of my flesh, but it was swift. And what was the suffering of my body compared to the violation of my soul?

My body thinned, became translucent. Light streamed through me. The sound of their merriment faded. I uncoiled from my prison and became lighter, so light I no longer felt anything. I know longer *was*.

I embraced myself.

Then I was gone, and only sea foam remained to mark my passing.

"Pink."

Yes. Perfect.

Just like in the movies, the black and white plants transform into an array of vibrant colors. Roses that were grey become red, and thistles of grass are painted green.

Where did the buildings go? Did the entire city disappear? I think about the old man, the teenagers, and the men in the white suits. I must be dreaming. That is the only explanation for the odd random occurrences and my ability to speak.

"Wake up!" I yell, but nothing happens.

Instead, my ears vibrate from the high volume. The sound pinballs around as if I am in a small room.

A purple butterfly passes within a few inches of my nose, and I realize I've created a place of complete serenity. All the evil has been pushed out, recycled into something useful. Something beautiful.

"Don't be afraid," I hear a voice say, but this time it's not mine.

"We can help you understand."

I turn around to see the white suits. I don't know how, but they found me.

"We've been through this, too. The experience is jarring, confusing beyond measure. We offer clarity."

There are three of them, but I hear more voices. Hundreds, maybe thousands. Their mouths move together, the words spoken in perfect synchronicity.

"Where..." The word chokes in my throat. I'm still learning to command my voice. "Where am I?"

"It is your palette, the place where it all begins," they reply. "You are special."

Lies. I've been tortured my whole existence, unable to convey my thoughts to the masses. Ridiculed, bullied, and misunderstood. Sometimes I discovered a compassionate soul, but often only apathy — the most dangerous drug of all. The poison of the uncaring.

"It's easier if we show you."

They spread their hands out and then clap them together. The hair on my skin stands up from the sound of thunder. The garden disappears. I float in blackness, surrounded by bright specks of distant light. I reflexively gasp for air, but realize I have no need of it. I am in space, surrounded by the infinite stretch of the universe. Instead of the white suits, I see the old man again. He smiles at me, and I feel warmth burning my insides like a hefty dose of whiskey going down the esophagus.

"My time is up," he coughs. "It's your turn to take my place." His voice is gravelly, and the pain he experiences is evident with each spoken syllable.

"Look."

He points downward, and I see it. White clouds, blue seas, and different colored lands. It's all there in a giant ball.

"It's yours," he says.

"I still don't understand," I reply.

"You... created... it."

Two of the white suits appear next to the man, holding his arms steady. He looks ready to collapse. None of this makes sense. I'm an accountant, not a god.

"We are creators," the old man manages to say.

"Of what?"

"Everything," the suits say. "Your world, your history... it never existed until you took your first breath. You created all of it in your infancy. Like a child learning to play with his toys, you learned to create your world. You lived in it as you formed it, but that world was never meant to be permanent. It was created based on the spark of another embedded inside you from birth."

They both glance at the man in the middle.

"But I have no memory of doing anything."

"No, you wouldn't. The early years are a training ground. An experiment. When you woke up this morning, echoes of your creation came back to you."

"What does this mean? What am I supposed to do?"

"Create. Live among them. Learn from them. Guide them."

"What about him?"

"His world destroyed itself. He is tied to his creation, as we all are. He will die, but not before he passes on his memories."

The old man reaches out his decrepit hand with one finger stretched out farther than the rest. I mirror his movement, only steadier... stronger. I feel a wave of images wash over me. They assert themselves into my consciousness faster than I should be able to comprehend, yet the memories align themselves in the compartments of my mind without confusion.

My world was much like his, populated by many of the same names and faces. Somewhere, its people took a wrong turn, and they chose self-destruction.

"Please," the old man says, "don't... repeat... my... mistakes."

The suits let him go, and he vanishes as if he never was. They look me in the eyes but say nothing. Then they shoot off in opposite directions at speeds incomprehensible to a normal man.

That is something I no longer am.

I squeeze my hands shut, balling them up into fists. I'm back in my garden an instant later. Water droplets hit the top of my head, and the colors mix together into a goopy mess.

Time to start over. Time to create a new world — a new beginning.

Perhaps I am not just an accountant after all.

Secret of the Springs
Patrick Neal

Acknowledgments:
I dedicate this story, intertwined with my past, to the four winds. May it be carried beyond the sea, beyond earth, and into the sun's fiery corona.

Chapter One:
A Squad of Bandits

It's always good to know where your roots lie. It's rather funny how when I drive back through the dusty old town of Center Point, Texas, it all seems much smaller than it did back then. As a child growing up there, it all seemed so large. From the old, abandoned house across the street that was kept tidy by Ms. Kline, to our backyard overlooking the horse pasture. That was our world and we would run the streets from sunup to dusk, ganking jerky snuff cans and Garbage Pail Kids stickers from the local Mini Mart – aka 'Stop n' Rob' – and going to the Lion's Park Dam. Later we'd accept punishment for getting into trouble. But trouble was what we were all about. The four of us, three brothers and best friend Ron Melton would elect the leader for the day and venture off somewhere. One warm summer day back in 1983, we decided to go to the Springs, a local swimming hole fed by a cold, underground water source. At the bottom of this particular spring lies a blue hole. Year after year, juniors and seniors challenge each other to dive to the bottom and back on one breath. So far, no one has been able to reach the bottom.

Cory, Pat, and Bill walked down shadow's eve. The trees lined the quiet street that led to Ron's house. Cory, eager to get things going, pushed open the rusty gate of his house. They

walked up the rocky driveway and the front door was open.
    Without knocking, Cory entered and Pat and Bill eagerly followed. There in the kitchen adjacent to a floor radiator, Ron was making bologna sandwiches for the trip. Cory walked up and chuckled as he stuffed a sandwich in his mouth and saved the rest in his shirt pocket. Ron then reached in the fridge and brought out pieces of raw bacon. He gave some to Cory and Pat and watched them both eat it.
    "You can get Trichinella from raw pork," Pat said, disgusted by the thought of eating raw meat.
    "Nah-ah," Ron said.
    "Park!" Pat replied in angst.
    "Let's go. Emily and the chicks might be there," Bill said, walking in from the living room.
    Pat thought of April, Emily's best friend. Eager to go see her and her friends in their bathing suits, he grabbed a sandwich and Mr. Pibb from Ron's pea green fridge and nudged the screen door ajar with his knee. He walked out past the rusty gate towards the road that led to the Springs. Bill came marching after him and Cory and Ron followed.
    "This is like Stand By Me," Pat mentioned.
    "Yeah, if we find a dead body then we get famous," Bill declared with delusions of grandeur.
    "Hey guys, wait up!" a familiar voice shouted behind them. They all looked back and saw it was Clay Bennington, the brothers' next door neighbor.
    "Aww, you said you weren't gonna invite him!" Pat whispered scornfully to Ron.
    "Shut up. he'll run home before the sun goes down. He's a mama's boy," Ron replied, quietly chuckling.
    Claybenerd Abenerd been a turd!" Pat said tauntingly.
    "Shut up, he gives me milk money!" Cory whispered.
    Pat hushed up and took the lead as Clay caught up and frowned at him.
    "I'm the yeader of you, you, and you," Clay said, pointing at each of them.
    Ron and Cory smirked at each other and Pat and Bill walked side by side. Clay found the muddy hill path that led to the Springs. They followed, trying not lose their footing on the

slippery embankment. There before them was the river that led to the hidden water hole.

Clay ran and jumped off the bank and grabbed a rope tied high in a tree. He clung like Tarzan and let go, hitting the water with a splash.

He swam arm over arm, throwing Cory the rope. Cory backed up a bit then lifted his feet and swung out above the water. He let go as he grabbed his shins and did a spinning cannonball before landing in the water. Cory threw Bill the rope and Bill grabbed it and ran along the shore before picking up his legs and swinging out in a semicircle over the water. When he let go, he did a side spin he learned in diving class. Bill threw the rope to the last person standing there, his younger brother Pat.

Pat grabbed the rope and fear sunk in his stomach as he saw his reflection ripple in the water.

"Do it you sissy, or I'm gonna tell April you like her," Bill teased his brother.

Pat summoned his courage and grabbed the rope as he ran towards the edge. He closed his eyes and copied his brothers, lifting his legs. He swung out over the water, clinging to the rope for dear life. He swung back and forth, hesitating to let go. The others laughed as they swam downstream. Finally, his hands began to burn and the fear of being left behind was more than he could bear so he let go, splashing into the cold river. He submerged, filling his cheeks with air as he rose to the surface. Gasping, he saw the others way ahead of him downstream, laughing and splashing at each other. Pat swam with urgency and finally caught up with them.

They made it to the secret spot, but there was an old man tending a wooden fence on the land just past the bank.

"This is my property, but you are welcome to swim here," the old man said.

"Thanks!" Ron turned his head to reply, but the old man was gone. They all looked around, dumbfounded at the old man's disappearance.

Pat swam above the blue hole, beckoning below like a jeweled mouth awaiting its next meal. Fear sank in his stomach and he got slightly panicky as he made it across and latched onto a tree root. Bill took a deep breath and dove down, his feet sticking out of the water for a moment before he went deeper. Ron huffed and took a breath and plunged down to try to race him in a torrent of bubbles. Cory held his nose and followed them down to the bottom of the blue hole.

Pat watched as they descended, looking like toy divers as the sunlight shone down the crystal-clear water. Bill looked up and gestured for Pat to follow.

Fear of many things belonged to Pat, but fear of drowning was absolutely the worst. Yet he felt obligated to man up, or they would tell April about the crush he had on her. So Pat let go of the root, drifted over the ominous blue hole and took what he thought might be his last breath and flipped upside down, head first into the water. He opened his eyes underwater and it stung a bit at first, but that soon subsided as he swam down the depths, eager to catch up and prove himself.

The deeper they went, the more it looked cavernous. Bill, more of an experienced swimmer because of his diving class, swam like a fish towards the opening of a cavern, emanating a blue light from an unknown source. Pat, living out one of his worst fears and running out of breath, decided to return to the surface.

The others didn't take notice as they followed Bill into the underwater cavern. Ron saw an air pocket above him and breached to take a breath of stale air, probably decades old. Cory's head popped up from the surface of the water next to him.

"He's crazy. I don't know how he can hold his breath so long. He's gonna drown. We should turn back," Ron said, his voice sounding like he was talking in a barrel.

"Yeah, let's live to tell the tale," Cory said before taking a deep breath and submerging once more. He swam out of the mouth of the underwater cavern.

Ron looked back into the pulsating lit cavern one last time before seeing Pat's distorted image standing above as they fought for the surface.

No matter how much of a man you are, you still need to breathe.

They fought for the surface like mad as they began to run out of oxygen. Pat, seeing their distress, dove in and grabbed the tree roots with one hand and with his other, pulled them up as they took gasping breaths, coughing.

"Where's Bill? He's still down there!" Pat asked, fearing the worst.

"He swam ahead of us towards the light," Ron gasped between breaths.

Cory acknowledged them with a nod, trembling as he sat on the bank with his feet in the water. The boys silently waited around the blue hole for Bill to surface.

Bill, however, swam further into the cavern, drawn by the pulsating blue light. His lungs burned but he fought it by thinking of food, a trick Coach Garza taught him. The cavern gradually became more and more illuminated and he noticed the surface of the water, glimmering in the sunlight in a rocky embankment. He surfaced and took a much-needed breath. He opened his eyes and saw beyond the rocky cove a place he had never seen: a forest with exotic looking plants.

"Must be private property," he said to himself as he climbed onto the rocks dripping wet as he ventured into the primeval looking forest.

He looked up and the branches above him were covered in a thick web-like material. The sunlight from above cast a silhouette of a big spider through the semi-transparent web. Bill didn't like spiders of any sort, especially ones that big, so he picked up the pace and ran through the forest, trying to find the fence to get out and back to the blue hole where he knew they were waiting. Trees seemed to reach out and smack him. A branch lashed out and cut his chest as he was ensnared by thorny vines. He tried to free himself, but the more he struggled, the tighter the vines coiled around his ankles and dug into his skin.

Supremely annoyed but not outdone, as he surely encountered weeds before from living on a farm, though none like these, he stopped to observe his surroundings. He saw a triangular rock poking out of the thick spiky vines that seemed to writhe and weave themselves tighter. He lunged for the stone and grabbed at it. Fortunately, it came loose in his hand. He used it to free himself from the vines.

His legs, bloody with scratches, seared a fleeting sense of victory before he caught a glimpse of what looked like Emily and April running through the forest. He followed them through the maze of twisted thorny cruel vines, the girls laughing as they looked back at him. Then, suddenly at a fork in the path, they split up, one going left and one going right. He followed the girl with dark brown hair like April's – he was almost sure that it was her. The other girl shouted in another language he had never heard before. He ran through the path and lost them over a hill as their laughter echoed through the forest. He stopped to catch his breath and just over the hill was a small village with thatched conical roofs. The people were dressed in forest-gathered materials, woven leaves and vines. He thought this was a hippy commune or some historical reenactment.

    The villagers looked at him, unsure of him, yet they were also curious about his attire.

    He figured they were wondering, "Who is this strange man wandering through our village?"

    He walked slowly through the strange village that seemed out of place, seeing a short elderly woman with hair that looked like a straw thatched roof. She stared at him and then scowled. Suddenly two men holding spears approached him. One put his hand on his shoulder. Figuring the was a reenactment, he grabbed the man's hand and twisted it. The man howled in pain and sank to his knees.

    Bill let go and the man cowered, with the other man helping him, giving him an unsure look. The surrounding forest began to shake as women appeared from its reaches, dressed in etched leather armor with swords drawn.

    "I am in heaven," Bill said under his breath.

    "You speak the language of the old ones," the leader of the female warriors said. She wore a metal helmet with a ridge down the nose with two almond shaped eyelets.

    "I'm not sure who the old ones are, but my name's William. You can call me Bill."

    The leader took off her helmet, freeing her stark white long hair. She had a face of beauty, bearing the scars of many battles. On her arms were metal arm bracers, etched with a symbol of a bird with curved talons.

    "Well, Bill, you can tell me all about how you crossed the threshold over a meal. My name's Spectra. My sisters Lozen and Asherah are famished from the hunt. Join us!" she said, gesturing with her hand as she led him to the center of the village where a fire was burning and a large stew pot boiled away, emitting vapors into the air.

    Bill sat on a stump next to a woman sitting Indian style, weaving something out of multicolored strands of some type of ornamental leaves, her face painted in an articulate design resembling a mandala. She smiled and continued stitching. He was then greeted by Spectra, holding a steaming bowl fashioned from a gourd. He took it and the steam hit his nose. It smelled amazing, and his stomach was growling. He used a wooden spoon like the others but instead of savoring it, he wolfed it down. The elders and tribeswomen all looked at him in shock.

    Lozen and Asherah laughed as they spoke in their language of an unknown dialect. He was pretty sure what they were talking about.

    "Okay, enough's enough. You can tell the girls you had me for a second, well maybe a minute. End the charade, I know you got these costumes from theater arts," Bill said, feeling Spectra's armor.

    It felt cold as he ran his fingers along the engravings. He withdrew his hand and noticed blood on his fingers and blood spattered on her breastplate.

    "Real enough for you?"

    "Well, I'm from earth. I come from this little town called Center Point. Nothing really goes on there unless you know the right people," he said nervously in a country accent as one of the warriors caressed the nape of his neck with her hand.

    "And where is this Center Point?" Spectra asked intently as other women warriors began to touch him.

    Blushing, he didn't know what to say. Back home, he'd never get this kind of attention from any girl, let alone any kind of contact.

    "I swam through the blue hole to get here. Looks like my friends didn't follow-"

    "Your friends? There are more of you?" Spectra interrupted him.

    "Yes," he said hesitatingly.

    "Show me where you entered our world and you can have whatever you wish," Spectra said with pouting lips.

Bill's heart raced at the temptation of so many beautiful women that were into him. His thoughts raced also and he thought of his friends that probably thought he was dead by now, drowned in the depths of the blue hole.

"Sounds very tempting but I must be going now," he said hurriedly.

"Why leave when you can have any desire you wish?" Spectra asked as one of the women warriors planted a kiss directly on his lips.

The subtle touch of her kiss was beyond anything he had ever experienced back home. None of the girls wanted to do that with him or his best friends, who were considered dorks and outcasts. The girls only preferred jocks. For a moment, he allowed himself to indulge and kissed her back. He closed his eyes and euphoric tingles radiated through his body like a jolt of electricity. He then felt like he had two tongues in his mouth. He opened his eyes and saw that the woman kissing him actually had a forked tongue. He recoiled and suddenly her face contorted to an evil expression with pointy teeth. He pushed her away and began running for the spring. He looked back and saw them in their true forms, hideous features morphed from their convincing disguises. Some flew after him with transparent wings and claws holding studded maces and swords.

"Why not stay for the main course?" Spectra asked in a gravelly tone, smiling and showing her jagged teeth. She then let out a maniacal laugh as she splayed her lengthy fingers, adorned with sharp talons like a bird's.

Without thinking, he jumped into the blue hole that he came from. He swam into the cave just as the sisters also dove in after him and Asherah latched on to one of his ankles. He bubbled in despair as he kicked free of her grasp. He swam faster than ever before, his heart racing and muscles burning. He looked back and didn't see them. He turned and Lozen's swirling dark hair ensnared him. He tried to swim free, but became entangled in her hair. Fearing the worst was about to come true, he yanked hard and ripped some of her hair out, kicking free of her deadly embrace. She screamed, sending out a stream of bubbles. He saw the light ahead and pushed on, using every ounce of energy to escape.

Finally, the end of the underwater chasm was in sight. He swam upwards but was caught by something sharp in his calf - Spectra's fingers that now resembled talons. He kicked her and got free and swam for the surface. His mind began playing tricks on him as he ran out of oxygen. He looked below him and instead of seeing the evil faeries, he saw April Andrews in a bathing suit.

"Don't you want to stay with me? Come back and you can have any desire," her voice entered his mind.

He recognized the tone, it was Spectra.

Shaking free from the illusion in a plume of bubbles, he gathered what little sense he had while time was running out to make a final fight for the surface, ascending fast. He glanced below and the faeries retreated back into the blue hole.

Chapter Two:
Erroneous Liaison

He finally breached the surface just before blacking out. Chest heaving, he climbed out on the tree roots and gathered his senses, reviewing the memories of his encounter with the faeries. He knew that if he told anyone, his friends would think he was crazy and he would be ridiculed at school. But that was no different from what he was receiving on a daily basis, so why keep quiet?

An impure thought entered his mind;
I'd love to see those jocks April and her friend are in love with go down the blue hole and get eaten by the faeries.

He gazed at the blue sky, a sky he was relieved to be under. He got up and walked home. Upon arriving, he saw his stepdad was on another one of his drunk tirades about being in the French Foreign Legion, singing in French. Bill ignored him and went to the room he shared with Cory, Pat, and Jimmy. Jimmy, his stepfather James' eldest, was obliviously playing Super Mario Brothers on an old TV they got from their grandparents. Cory was lying in his top bunk bed with his feet on the ceiling. Pat came in and was shocked to sees his brother, believed to have drowned in the blue hole.

"Bill, you're alive!" Pat shouted.

Cory sat up and looked as their mother, Sandra, came storming in. She gave him a hug and checked him over.

"Where have you been? They've been looking all over. We thought you drowned trying to show off to your friends," his mother declared with worry etched in her forehead.

"You'll never believe me. Please don't tell dad!" Bill pleaded.

"I won't, but I know when you're hiding something, you get that blinky eye," his mom sighed in relief that he was okay.

"Well I thought it was a prank at first, but they're pretty real. Faeries – evil ones. Through the Springs. They can disguise themselves to look like someone else to lure people like me," Bill

said in one breath.
"For what? What would a grown woman want with a cheeky boy like you?" she asked in a smarty tone, pinching his left cheek.
"Ow! I tell you they're real. They wanted to eat me. They offered me food at first, but then she said I was on the menu! Her face changed from pretty to disgusting real quick," Bill said, going into the kitchen for some red Kool-Aid.
"Sounds like a real bitch. Did they hurt you?" she asked, examining his jaw, scraped up from the encounter with the faeries.
"Luckily, no but they were very interested in seducing me," Bill said, sipping his Kool-Aid and staining his lips red.
"Allouette, gentille allouette! Allouette, je te plumerai!"
James stumbled in drunk, wearing a cowboy hat and jeans and a western style shirt. His eyes opened wide when he saw Bill standing in the doorway to the kids' bedroom.
"Bill here has quite a story. He says evil faeries tried to seduce him and then tried to eat him." Sandra said, looking down at Bill.
Bill, embarrassed by looking like he made the story up, went outside to get a breath of fresh air. He heard them shouting at each other and James went to the master bedroom and slammed the door shut. Sandra came into the boys' bedroom, shaken up after dealing with her drunk husband reliving his days as a paratrooper.
His stepdad told her Bill needed to see a shrink. He also forbade him from talking about this any further under penalty of a belting.
"Go to bed, we'll talk about this in the morning with Dr. Fletcher," Sandra said to him through the screen and went to her bedroom where James was, lying down on the bed still in his clothes and reminiscing his glory days. She closed the door.
Bill slipped into his PJs and went to bed, images of the hideous man-eating fairies' faces raced through his mind. A thousand thoughts whirled around his brain until he drifted off to sleep.
He dreamt he was swimming in the blue hole, the gemstone walls of the chasm emanating the deep blue drew him further, back to

the cove where he encountered the evil faeries.

He slowly lifted his head out of the water. Realizing he was dreaming, he wished he had wings and could fly. Something wriggled in his upper back and wrought-iron wings formed on his shoulder blades. He willed for them to work as they fluttered rapidly, lifting him high into the cool midnight air, high above the trees, waving with their leaves. He zoomed over rolling hills and jagged mountain teeth until arriving at the faerie village. He touched down onto the soft dirt. The smell of a dead fire loomed in the air. He looked around and all the faeries were gone and all was quiet except the willful chirps of crickets. He peeked inside a hut and heard an awful snoring. Inside was a faerie in its true form, long angular bluish face and sunken eyes. He checked all the huts and all were occupied by sleeping faerie except one: the leader Spectra's bed was empty. He flew around looking for her, but couldn't find her in the darkness of the dreamworld. He became afraid that if he didn't get back to his body in time, that his body would die and he would be cursed to haunt the land of the faeries for eternity. He flew back to the cove where the blue hole was. He plunged into the icy water and swam, using his iron wings to propel himself through the underwater cavern, back to his world. On the way up, he woke up.

    Bill gasped as he looked around the bedroom, Cory was still asleep, his mouth hung open as he snored in the predawn. Jimmy and Pat were also still sleeping. He looked at the clock and it was ten minutes 'til seven, when mom would come in and wake everyone up for school. He got up quietly and got dressed, tiptoeing out into the kitchen and carefully opening the fridge door. He grabbed the jug of milk and drank from it, despite the countless times his parents told him not to mouth the milk jug. The cold milk numbed his esophagus and he carefully capped it and set it back in the fridge, awaiting the next unsuspecting sibling or parent to use it for cereal or coffee, completely unaware it now had his cooties.

    There was no time, so he grabbed a biscuit and stuffed it in his pocket and went out the back door, softly closing it behind him as he stepped lightly towards the back gate. Rather than opening it and alerting anyone, he climbed over and walked across the street to Ron's aunt Louise's trailer. He stepped up on the wooden porch and knocked on the door.

    Ron opened the door and the smell of fried bacon wafted

out. Bill walked in and sat on the couch as Ron presented him with a piece of crispy bacon. Bacon wasn't allowed at home since his stepfather was practicing Judaism, so this was a rare treat. He scarfed it down and went to the fridge to grab some OJ. Ran sat next to him and liberally doused his scrambled eggs with ketchup. He began to eat as Bill cleared his throat.

"Tomorrow night is the prom. I wanted to ask April, but I don't know what she'll say," Bill said, nervously tapping his fingers on the table.

"You get her a rose and give it to her, then just ask her." Ron said, sopping up the ketchup and eggs with a slice of bread.

"I feel if I showed her I could swim to the bottom of the blue hole and beyond, then she would think I'm a real man and go out with me."

"You could ask her to meet us there after school. If her friend brings that jock Matt, then you could race him to the bottom. You're a better swimmer than he is, no matter how good a football player he is." Ron suggested, throwing on his hoodie.

They set out for school, Bill knowing perfectly well that he was supposed to see the school shrink today. They arrived as breakfast was being served. Bill went through the line and got a trey, loading up with cereal and juice. Ron met him at the tables and they ate the cereal dry. Then Ron chugged the milk until the carton imploded. After the buses arrived, time ticked away and the bell rang. Everyone shuffled off to their first class of the day. Bill walked to the attendance office where Dr. Fletcher was at his desk, reviewing his notes.

"Ah, Mr. Cummings, I've been expecting you. Please sign in on the pamphlet," Dr. Fletcher said, eyeing his handwriting behind rectangular glasses.

"So what's been bothering you? Your mother told me you see faeries," Dr. Fletcher continued, scribbling on paper.

"The blue hole, the spot where everyone goes to swim. It is a porthole to another world where they exist," Bill said nervously.

"And what do these faeries look like?" the doctor asked, glancing at him behind his reading glasses and back to his notes.

"At first, beautiful. Then they make you eat something and then their mirage wears off. It was like the meal made me see their true form."

"And what, pray tell, did they feed you?" The doctor asked as he stopped writing.

"I don't know, but whatever it was, tasted better than the cafeteria. I felt hungry so I ate it," Bill said, as Spectra viewed them in her crystal ball, overhearing their whole conversation.

Just then, Bill got a ringing in his ear. He bit his tongue and the ringing slowly dissipated.

"Are you alright Bill? Should we continue at another time?" Dr. Fletcher asked, seeing him flinch.

"No, it's all right. I narrowly escaped with my life – they were about to eat me."

Dr. Fletcher was silent as he scribbled on his notepad. He tore it off and handed it to him. It read, "Hall Pass."

"I will review this and let you know. Off you go now!" Dr. Fletcher said insistently.

Bill trotted off to class, where his crush, April, also had class. Mr. Diltz, the science teacher, was giving a lecture about the laws of motion. Bill found a seat right behind April. He stared at the back of her head, oblivious of what Mr. Diltz was saying.

"And what is the law of motion Bill?" Mr. Diltz asked, looming over Bill. The class laughed as Bill broke from his trance, looked up dumbfounded and replied, "Inertia?"

The whole class roared in laughter. Bill didn't care. He was glad to be the class clown. It broke up the monotony of living in this small town.

"Apparently, Bill is correct, as Newton's first law of motion is sometimes called the law of inertia," Mr. Diltz said, the bookworms making a note of it, scribbling it down in their notebooks.

The bell rang and everyone scrambled to their next class. On the way to math, Bill walked past April in a corridor. He tried to build the nerve to ask her, but he just looked at her quietly as she walked by, carrying her books.

Another opportunity just passed him by as he looked back to see her now talking to a football player, handing her a note. His stomach twisted as he somberly walked, hanging his head low and his pride lower. He eagerly went to math class, where it was more sterile.

Miss Chevet was a math teacher from France. Beautiful in every way, catching the eye of every adolescent male who was in the midst of puberty. He sat through class staring at her, admiring her form and wishing he was a bit older. He daydreamed a lot about things that would never happen. He turned in his homework and she smiled as she filed it away in her notebook.

She handed him a stack math tests and sweetly asked, "Do you mind handing these out for me?"

Bill jumped at the opportunity of being the teacher's pet and happily handed them out to everyone in the class. He sat down and began to work out the math problems, occasionally spying on another kid's answers and copying. He turned it in and waited in scribbling silence until the second bell rang.

Next class was gym, everyone's favorite nightmare. The day continued like any other, and finally there was lunch followed by recess.

On the playground, April and Matt, her prom date, were talking by the swing set. Bill summoned his courage and walked up to her. She stopped talking and looked at Bill with eyes that would make anyone surrender.

Bill cleared his throat and said, "Later, me and the guys are going out to the Springs. There's something I found down in the blue hole."

"I don't know, you?" April asked looking at Matt. Matt gave Bill a forced smile and said, "Sure. I've been meaning to check the place out."

"See you there after school. The old man that owns the land said it's okay if we go swim there," Bill said as he shook Matt's hand, his iron grip tightening around Bill's like a wrench before letting go.

Bill urgently walked away, shaking the life back into his hand and walked to the stone table where nerds hung out to play D&D. With the trap set with Matt as the bait, he felt he couldn't go wrong. He drifted off in thought.

April would fall for me for sure if I beat him to the bottom. Then let the faeries have him and he'll be out of the picture for good...

"Hey, snap out of it! You there?" Robby asked, waving his hand in front of Bill's eyes.

Bill sighed and got up to roam the halls until the bell rang for class to resume. The day played out like usual then the final bell rang, the one he'd been waiting for. He stormed home and got dressed, wearing his swim trunks under his shorts. He hobbled as he slipped his shoes on and anxiously walked the lonesome shady road to the Springs.

Along the way, a car sped down the road and honked. He looked inside the window and saw April sitting in the passenger's seat. His stomach sank as he picked up the pace, jogging on a trail that led to the blue hole. He dove in the river and waded downstream, seeing April and Matt parked up a hill just above the Springs. He wasted no time and swam to claim the spot before anyone else did so as to take the credit. He swam around the bend in the stream and his heart sank as he saw his friends Ron and Clay had beaten him to the spot. He quietly swallowed his pride and joined them in tossing a football around in the cold spring water.

"What's the matter, sissies, afraid you'll drown? Let me show you how it's done!" Matt said as he walked down the muddy bank and took his shirt off. Bill saw him flex his abs as April approved with a smile.

Matt dove into the water head first. Not to be outdone in front of the girl of his dreams, Bill kicked off his muddy shoes and shirt and dove into the ice-cold water. Bubbles streamed around him as he pushed himself to swim deeper into the frigid water. The rocky features stood out like faces of the damned, watching them swim to their doom as Matt found the cavern where the blue light was emanating from. Bill swam cautiously behind him as they swam through the cave, the pressure of the deep pushing on his eardrums. He held his nose and popped his ears, equalizing the pressure. Matt swam towards the rocky cove, seeing the light beckoning them like unsuspecting prey. Bill swam over Matt, kicking his head as he breached. He waited in still silence until Matt's head popped up.

"What's this place?" Matt asked, gasping for air.

"It's a secret place," Bill said as he got out of the water onto the rocky ledge that surrounded the cove. He offered his hand to help Matt up. Matt, soaking wet from the swim, raised his head and looked at Bill dead in the eye as he grasped his hand tightly.

Bill's knuckles popped in Matt's grasp. He yanked his hand free and backed up as Matt set foot on the soil leading into the forest.

"If this is some type of joke, believe me, you and your friends will be sorry!" Matt said, taking the lead through the dense forest.

Matt looked oddly at the bizarre branches and leaves resembling daggers.

"And another thing. Stop staring at April, it freaks her out. She's mine, understand?" he said, looking back at Bill.

Matt then turned around and stopped when he caught a glimpse of the tribe of women.

Bill smirked as he followed Matt towards the staked-off fence of the thatched roof village. He wandered in behind him, not afraid for his own life at the least. They were greeted by Spectra, who wore a headpiece with a jewel in the center of her forehead. Matt was transfixed by her and followed her to where Asherah and Spectra sat on a throne made from bones and skin. Spectra wore a white feathered hairpiece and held a spiky mace.

"You are either a fool or you want to pay with death by returning here. What's this morsel you bring me?" Spectra asked as she inspected Matt, drawing his attention to her.

"I want in return immortal life in exchange for this offering," Bill said to the sisters as they surrounded Matt, caressing him and entangling him in their spell.

"Yes, I will grant your wish." Spectra said as her face morphed from a beautiful woman warrior to her true face, contorted by evil and then back again.

Matt, spellbound by the attention from three lovely females, was oblivious as Spectra undid the clasp of her necklace holding a black shiny pendant.

She handed it to Bill and said, "Wear this jewel and thy will live forever."

Bill, inebriated by the thought of never having to die, eagerly took the pendant and strung it around his neck. The pendant twitched and from it sprang six tiny legs, sharp at the ends that stuck into his neck, attaching itself to him and burrowing into his skin. He sank to his knees as he struggled with the insect probing deeper into his body.

Matt snapped out of his trance as he saw Bill sitting there, a blank look in his eyes. He hung his head forward and collapsed in front of him. Matt, fully sober from the faeries' hypnotizing dance, shook his head and began to run back for the cove. He stepped over Bill's still body and Bill's hand suddenly reached up and grasped his ankle, firmly holding onto him. Matt kicked him off and stopped as Bill rose up from the ground with no effort, turning his back to him. The faeries, hungry and riled up, stopped their chase and watched with their hungry black eyes.

Matt's hand shook as he reached out to touch Bill's shoulder. It was ice cold, like the water. Bill turned around with a pale face as sinister as the evilest of faeries. His eyes and veins were as black as the pendant, now controlling him from within. He grabbed Matt's hand and gave it a squeeze that would crush any jocks' hand. Matt winced from the pain and yelled, knowing his throwing days were over after hearing his phalanges crunch and break. Matt freed his hand and limped toward the cove as the faeries circled around him, closing in.

Bill, now a man-eating faerie by default, splashed into the water after him as Matt dove into the icy blue. He saw their gnarly feet jumping in after him as he plunged into the blue hole. In a cascade of bubbles, he thought he had lost them as he swam through the cavern leading back to his world, avoiding the stalactites that resembled teeth. Suddenly the blue light dissipated and the ceiling and floor of the cavern began to close in on him.

"No way!" He thought as he saw what looked like a tongue rise up and cloud the water.

The cavern was no cavern at all, but a sleeping monster lying undisturbed, underwater for centuries. He narrowly made it out of the giant mouth as it closed behind him, nipping at his feet. Bubbles rose out of the cavern monster's mouth furiously. He turned around to look as he swam upwards. In the jail of the teeth was Bill in his human form fighting to get out. Matt knew what Bill was planning all along and swam to the surface.

April covered him in a towel as he took several breaths. In the dim light of day, surrounded by Cory, Ron and Clay, he told them what happened.

They thought he was delirious from oxygen deprivation and asked him about Bill.

"He's one of them now. You must never tell, keep this a secret!" Matt said as April helped him walk back to his truck.

"What are we gonna do? He probably killed Bill and made the story up!" Ron said.

"If what he says is true, then you boys can never tell anyone about this or the secret of the Springs will no longer be a secret!" the mysterious old man said, appearing from nowhere.

"Mister, how- where did you come from?" Cory asked.

"Let's just say it's a secret," the old man chuckled as he whistled a tune through his teeth, tending to the fence.

Hiding behind a cypress tree across the river was the school counselor Dr. Fletcher, secretly watching and listening to everything they said.

The End?

TALES FROM APPLEBOTTOM: VOL. 1
IT STREET

    The day began not unlike any other morning in the lively little hamlet of Applebottom - or at least, that's how it felt to Midas Bellview. Stepping out onto his front branch to take in the sunshine, Midas waved politely to the mother sparrow building a nest in the crook of the limb across from him, and - with a yawn far mightier than his size - stretched out his wings. The light autumn breeze felt cool and refreshing as it ran through the tiny hairs along the outer edge of his iridescent blue and gold-accented pinions.
    "Ah! Another great day to be a pixie!" he exclaimed gleefully to the world, and flew off to seize it with a big smile on his tiny face... a smile far too big for the events that fate had in store for him that day.
    It's not that Midas could be blamed for his optimism. Pixies, for the most part, are an unflappably positive lot - especially the Orchard pixies, of which Midas was one. Gregarious and profoundly social, Orchard pixies spent most of their days flitting from one tree village to another, engaging in lengthy discussions over the hues of their particular tree's apples with an overabundance of civic pride.
    "Lovely shade of red on the Crimson Suns this season, if I don't say so myself," Midas overheard one emissary boastfully boom as he weaved his way through the traffic of the Applebottom Trade Branch.
    It was here at the Trade Branch that the best apples of each tree were proudly displayed by that tree's emissaries, quite eager to extol the virtues of said fruit to the seemingly endless parade of traveling dust merchants ("dusters" to the locals) that buzzed around them. If a duster was particularly swayed by any of these overtures, the apple would be analyzed from stem to stern and a price would be suggested for core dust sampling. This often resulted in frantic, impromptu bidding wars, with

dusters from multiple villages wildly attempting to outbid the other for the first (and usually most potent) samples. Meanwhile, the tree's apple emissaries ruthlessly attempted to upsell their suddenly hot commodity and drive up the price of their apple stock by enticing other passing emissaries to bid.

This was viewed by all parties as an effective way of doing business.

When the final bid was cast, the winning parties would be allowed to sample the core until the apple was either fully drained of its essence or all bidders were satisfied. Money exchanged hands and dusters returned to their trees, where the dust was sold to the townsfolk and used for cooking, manufacturing, research, and creating shinier strains of apples to sell to other dusters.

However, ask any Orchard pixie and it will tell you that the most important use of the core dust samples is Pothan - a robust, potent, and incredibly addictive substance renowned for its transformative magical abilities, as well as its capacity to imbue those who consume it with a staggering sense of euphoria. Masters of their craft, Pothan Brewmasters can nimbly transmute their product into a litany of different potions, pastes, and powders, with flavors and effects as varied as the hues of the apples which produced them. New batches of Pothan are unveiled in massive tree-wide festivals that can last for days or even weeks, depending on the strain. Each strain is then named and classified in accordance with the highlights of the festivities in which it was introduced: names like "Midmonth Mothfire," "Dayflight Dream" and "the Dive Bomb" are enough to inflame the imaginations – and empty the pocketbooks – of prospective buyers.

Midas took a midflight sip of "Applebottom Unicycle Parade" (a favorite vintage from a festival from a few summers ago that held particularly fond - and fuzzy - memories) and slipped the tiny flask back into his pocket. A warm, ethereal glow came over him. His wings immediately felt lighter; fluttering faster and leaving behind a trail of glittering dust in the midday sun as he zipped away from the commotion of the Applebottom Trade Branch. The lightness in his flapping wings belied the seriousness of his demeanor as he sped off towards his destination: a tree on the far western edge of the Orchard hosting a village called Lefthouse.

Midas was heading to Lefthouse in his official capacity as a Pixie Cider Pothan Apple Core Brewing Process Quality Control Inspector ("Inspector" for short, or "PCPACBPQCI" for pixies who loved rattling off confusing-but-important-sounding jargon – and there were many who did). As an inspector, Midas had heard rumblings throughout the duster community that the Lefthousians had been dust-cutting their Pothan.

Dust-cutting was an uncommon but not unheard-of tactic where brewers would take the high quality core samples and cut them with rotten or spoiled cores of lesser quality apples in an attempt to boost production of an already successful Pothan recipe. These were serious allegations. A substandard Pothan could cause quite a literal headache for an unsuspecting pixie, resulting in a hangover that could last for days, along with some... well, let's just call them unexpected side effects. Even worse, if a pixie unsuspectingly dusted another creature in the Orchard with bad Pothan....

Midas shuddered at the thought. Pothan dust was commonly used by Pixies as a way of ensuring friendship with all nearby creatures. Creatures who saw pixies in their natural form immediately received a dusting of Pothan. Once dusted, those memories would be replaced by the sweet smell of cinnamon and thoughts of a pleasant, pixie-free stroll through the Orchard.

Humans were the pixies' greatest threat, so as humanity evolved, so too did the pixies' Pothan recipes, incorporating new features that continued to shield them from documentation. Snap a photo of a pixie, and the Pothan dust would obscure the image just enough to where the unwitting pixie was an incomprehensible blur – much like the memories of the pixies in the mind of the human taking the photo. For millennia, pixies had closely observed the rise of humanity and had seen enough to know that preserving their mythical status among the humans was, essentially, preserving their continued existence. It was a lesson taught to all Pixies from the moment they emerged from Chrysalis.

And yet, there were times when even the direst of warnings was not enough to prevent a harried brewmaster from pulling substandard core dust to make supply deadlines, even though it meant risking the potential exposure and eradication of the entire species – or even worse, the revocation of a brewmaster's license! That's why inspectors like Midas were present at each uncasking, and thereafter on call to resolve any complaints that arose.

Midas was fairly certain that was not the case with Lefthouse. He had presided over several of the tree's casking festivals in recent months and everything had always been above board. He knew many of the brewmasters on a first name basis - he was even Lindo Barksdale's pixie godfather, for crying out loud!

Surely this is just sour apples from a pixie who hit the dust too hard, he thought to himself.

Midas pulled up to the Lindo's Flights a'Fancy Brewery Lefthouse Trade Branch and almost immediately spied Vallen Thyme rubbing wings with a few dusters next to a large Golden Delicious that had sent the masses into near hysterics the previous morning. The sheen on the apple's skin was like staring into the Sun. Now, the dusters were tapping into its base, snaking their instruments through its juicy flesh to collect the surely exquisite dust that resided within its core.

When Vallen turned and saw Midas approaching, her smile made the apple look dull and lifeless by comparison.

"Midas!"

"Hey there, Vallen," Midas said, trying to sound as even as possible. "Good to see you, too. Is Lindo around? I reached out to him yesterday about the... well, the observation."

He mostly succeeded in staying on message, but the slightest hint of apology crept into his voice. *The observation*. He hated this part. He knew that it came with the job and that a rogue brewmaster could jeopardize the entire colony, but it had been so long since that had actually happened that most of these inquiries ended with nothing wrong. He fervently disliked the latent accusation that his presence created.

In a flash, Vallen's expression shifted from cheerful and bubbly to sort of manic professionalism.

"One second, Midas."

She tapped twice on her antennae, looked peeved, and

then tapped twice more.

"Hey Phil, is Lindo there? Yeah, I KNOW he's busy, but can ya get him to put down the freakin' mixer for a second and answer his pinger?"

Vallen mouthed something at Midas that looked vaguely like "UN – BELIEVABLLLLLLLE!" and rolled her eyes, then flashed back to business mode and tapped twice more on her antennae.

"Lindo! Move your flappers, fella! We got a P-C-P-A-C-B-P-Q-C-I here to do a Q-C-I-O-M-R on the L F-a-F!"

By the end of her alphabet soup, Vallen was talking so fast that the abbreviation for the brewery came out sounding like "elepha eff".

Midas wasn't eavesdropping on the conversation on purpose, but he was either close enough to where his antennae picked up the "Huh?" on the other end of the antennae, or Vallen's exasperated response was obvious enough to where he might as well have.

"Midas wants to see ya. Okay, sug – buh-bye now." She tapped her antennae twice and the smile returned. "Okay, dear," she said, turning to face Midas again., "he'll be right...."

The scream of terror that came out of Vallen's mouth was so sudden and unexpected that Midas almost fell off the branch. Her face was suddenly pale. She clasped her hands to her mouth, shaking, eyes fixed behind Midas into the field below.

Midas whirled around, and the scene that was playing out before his eyes stopped him cold. A massive figure stood by the Lefthouse tree, its face obscured by a mesh visor. Above the figure, swarms of Lefthousians were gathering in ramshackle attack formations and diving downward at the giant in waves, their Pothan-dipped spears glancing harmlessly off its thick brown armor. Other Pixies attempted to dust the goliath by buzzing around its face.

Meanwhile, another armored figure about half the giant's size swung at the Pixies with some sort of device Midas had never seen before. It resembled a Pixie spear, but it was much larger, and instead of a tip, it bore a gaping maw made from the same mesh material as the larger behemoth's visor.

The smaller one swung the weapon into the swarm,

snaring a Lefthousian warrior unable to swerve quickly enough to escape. The poor wretch was then quickly covered from escape by a giant, armored paw. The smaller giant uttered a deafening exclamation that sounded like – was it glee? Whatever it was, it sent chills right through to the tips of Midas' wings. Without thinking, he grabbed his pouch of dust and sped towards the melee below.

The larger figure turned towards its protégé and booming out its approval, then stepped over to a nearby table and it opened what appeared to be a massive briefcase. Its contents were too grotesque for Midas to immediately process, but when he did, his blood ran cold.

Up and down the interior of the case were the bodies of Pixies, splayed out and mercilessly run through with massive steel bolts in some sort of perverse array. As Midas watched from above in silent horror, the massive figure reached into the netting, pulled out the screaming, struggling pixie, and, without hesitation, impaled his left wing to the board. The Pixie's eyes went wide in terror and pain and he began clawing at his attacker. Unfazed, the giant ran a second dagger through the pixie's right wing. Midas could see his poor countryman rip through his own flesh to attempt to escape - attempts that were sharply ended with a shuttering jerk when the figure rammed a third bolt through the pixie's midsection. With one final desperate act of defiance, the crucified Lefthousian warrior grabbed the bolt that ran him through, tried to pull it out, and breathed his last; his blood-covered hands still gripping the instrument of his demise.

***

Mark Hinojosa squinted through the mesh of his beekeeper's mask at the latest treasure in his collection. Though entomology had been a passion of his for decades now, he'd never seen anything quite like this. These little creatures were certainly as ornery as any yellowjacket colony he'd encountered - the reception he'd received as he approached the tree made him thankful that he'd decided on the protection of his beekeeping suit before setting foot in the orchard. And yet, despite their aggressiveness, their big, bright wings were usually markers of more cooperative, peaceful species. As stunning as the designs on their wings were, it was their variety that truly captured Mark's attention. Pink and green, red and white, purple and orange - clearly each of these butterflies was from the same genus and species, but the complexity of their wing patterns was far more diverse than a typical Monarch butterfly or a Death's Head moth. Each set of wings had its own specific color scheme and style - almost like a snowflake, or a fingerprint....

"Dad! Dad! I got another one!"

Mark turned from his collection, chuckling at the beaming smile emanating from behind the mesh mask beside him.

"Good job, Matty!" Mark exclaimed, stooping down to examine the boy's latest prize. "Oh - blue and gold! How pretty!"

Mark grabbed another set of pins from the stack. He was initially worried about how Matty would react to his hobby - bug collecting can seem a little morbid at first - but the boy's enthusiasm and curiosity were infectious. And it turned out he was surprisingly skilled with a butterfly net as well.

Maybe I have a little aspiring bugcatcher on my hands, he thought proudly. He looked inside the net at Matty's latest catch. Another specimen, another set of markings. Fascinating. He took the tiny creature from out of the net and grabbed the pins.

"Dad?" Matty stopped his father with the question. "Can I keep this one?"

Mark smiled, reached into the bottom of his collection case, pulled out a mason jar with some holes in the lid, and handed it to his son.

"Sure, Matty. Just be sure to leave it water and nectar. You wouldn't want it to starve - that'd be cruel."

Matty took the mason jar and carefully slid the blue-and-gold insect inside, then shut the lid.

"He doesn't like nectar, Dad," Matty corrected. "He likes apples."

Mark chuckled as the two of them removed their masks and began the long walk towards the orchard entrance. "Does he now?" quizzed Mark playfully. "How do you know that? And for that matter, how do you know that *it* is a *he* at all?"

"He told me," Matty stated matter-of-factly.

Matt laughed and playfully tussled the boy's hair,

brushing off the thin, stray wisps of pollen that had collected around his shoulders. A subtle, almost indiscernible scent filled the air. Cinnamon? Mark took a deep breath. There was just something magical about this orchard.

"So," Mark inquired, "what are you going to name this little friend of yours?"

"Midas," Matty replied. "Midas Bellview.

THE SENTINEL
MICHAEL WIGINGTON

Deacon closed his eyes and listened to the engine idling for a brief moment. The Hellion went silent as his thumb hit the kill switch. It was a two-wheeled remnant from an older time and held together from parts he had scrounged. He had his own special brew to fuel the beast. He loved to tinker with it and get lost in his own thoughts.

Now all thoughts turned to Sylvia.

Slipping off the bike, he removed his jacket and ran a slender finger across the blades that lined his chest. A dozen flat-black knives. Razor-edge points that had finished many of the Altered. The same set his father had forged for him many years ago.

Thwack, thwack, thwack.

He could hear them to this day sinking into the moving targets his father had set up. Fifteen years later and the man's instructions still rang in his head.

"Duck, throw, jump, throw, dodge. Speed, boy. Speed wins the day. We can remake this world, Deacon, but we'll have to fight for it."

The street was empty, but they were here. He knew it. Old Jon Tarks, bruised and bleeding, had told him they headed south towards Breckenbury. The fucks had taken Sylvia. His one, his lady, his last rose of summer. She was the only thing in this world worth fighting for. Sylvia loved him when no one else would. She put up with his idiosyncrasies and when the *Darkness* came over him, she always saw him through it. Together they had forged a home, forged a community. Northhaven, they called it. A place to settle and raise children, a safe place to live, or so he thought.

Northhaven, the beginning of the remaking of the world. The joy he had felt when he stood before the small village and proclaimed his love for her, and she for him. Their wedding. Sylvia *was* Northhaven. It would be nothing without her.

Thunder vibrated tin roofs of ramshackle houses as if metal gods descended, bringing him out of his thoughts. Dark clouds loomed as light rain fell from the sky and steam blanketed the street.

He placed a thumb to one nostril, blew, and then checked the leather-handled blade across his back, more of a long knife than anything; his back up. Taking a deep breath, he hung his goggles on the clutch handle and ran a hand through his shock of bone-white hair. Rain fell harder, streaking his leather pants.

"Deacon." She planted a soft kiss on his lips. *"I can take care of myself. The Sentinel will warn us ahead of time should any trouble come, and I have the gun. Now go."* Her smile touched her big brown eyes as dark curls lapped at pale shoulders.

He had gone out on a supply run and come back to ruin. They all felt so safe, with their walls, early warning signal, and makeshift guns. The Sentinel had failed. A few of the Altered met their demise at the barrel of her gun. They must have had more numbers than usual for the weapon lay on the ground where she had made her stand.

Now, everything turned to shit. A raw deal.

Many had made it into the Haven. Those that did not were claimed as slaves. Many who fought back were rotting. Some elderly, though beaten and bloody, remained to tell the story.

Their locked hidey-hole would run short of food before too long and none who could get out of Haven had made it in. Deacon released a white-knuckled fist as frustration raged through him. As if he did not have enough to worry with Sylvia stolen, but now it was up to him or Phantom Jack to find one of the 'keys.' They had all been captured, unbeknownst to the creatures that took them. Of course, finding Sylvia would solve both of his problems. Jack had said he would go southwest and see if any had gone to the old city of Goldglen, a favorite raiding spot for Tyrant, near Wasteland the area the Altered called home.

Deacon had lost radio contact with Jack miles back. He was on his own.

Sylvia was not dead. Not yet. He had time if he could get to Tyrant and make a trade. Flesh was his biggest commodity and these fucks were his errand boys. Tyrant always traded but he moved from place to place. Deacon had to find him before he traded her and they would know where to find him.

A faded and rusted-out *Welcome to Breckenbury* sign half-rested on the ground, the other half clung to an old crumbling brick pillar. A different time and age. Deacon gave a brief pause for that time in human history. What must it have been like to live in relative peace. He was born after that golden age. Before it all fell apart as fire blazed in the sky and desolation struck the Earth. Before men no longer cared for the rule of law.

"There is only one law, now, Deacon. Might makes right. Remember that," his father said, poking him in the chest.

The town – what was left of it – appeared to have been a small, quaint place. A cathedral stood stark against the sky. Upturned skeletons of burned out rusting cars littered the pavement. Cobbled together fences, offering scant protection, divided some of the houses. A cackle of shrill laughter echoed from up the street. That is where they were, hiding their numbers. The laughter sounded again.

Such a waste. Ruin wrought not of their own making.

They attacked in groups and killed without mercy, stole people, food, butchered livestock, took their human spoils to Tyrant and then skulked back to the ruins to eat and rut. Even their Smallings, as their offspring were called, were feral. How they ever learned to speak was beyond Deacon. But talk they could, and talk they would, even though it might take you awhile to get anything that made sense.

"Come on out, you fucks!" Deacon spat as he walked up street. "We need to talk, and I know you won't do it the easy way."

Dogs whined behind a wooden fence.

A cathedral bell sounded in the distance.

The Altered filed out from behind the ruined vehicles. Two big Brutes wielding iron bars stood behind five cadaverous Freaks. Seven of them. One of them would give him the information he sought.

Seven, though. He had fought them before, sometimes two

at a time. Three would prove a challenge, and seven might prove lethal.

We do what we must, Deacon. Don't try to process it, just flow. Their moves, your moves, it's all a dance, boy. Dance, his father instructed.

He had danced so many times since then.

Tattered and torn clothes clung to their flesh. Lank, long hair hung in patches from their skulls. Red-pupiled eyes stared at him.

Silence fell as the cathedral bell ended its chime.

They charged, shrieks and cries pouring from their rotted mouths. The Brutes, with heavy steps, lumbered behind the others.

Hand outstretched, Deacon motioned them forward with two fingers. "Closer, bitches. That's it. Come and get it."

Closing the gap, the Freaks leapt. Thin fingers with long ragged nails descended towards him.

Hands blurred as knives twitched from them. Four black blades whispered into the air and hurtled towards his attackers. He ducked, drew more knives from their sheaths and rolled forward. One of the Freaks hit the ground, dead, steel impaled in its skull. Another clutched at its throat as blood washed down yellow skin. A third pulled at the blade that had blossomed in its chest and sank to the ground. The fourth yanked a knife from its shoulder and joined the fifth as they slid on wet pavement. They turned and charged again.

The Brutes closed in.

He would be between the hammer and the anvil soon.

He needed to keep one of these things alive.

Rain poured from the sky, making for uncertain footing. Sprinting as much as the rain allowed, he charged the big beasts.

"A kitten comes to play," laughed one of them. "Come to scratch us with your claws, little kitten?"

Deacon slid under a swinging iron bar and embedded a knife into a thick thigh.

The Brute cried out as he sank to one knee. The wet pavement carried Deacon past his attackers as the remaining ones gave chase.

Pushing up, Deacon rose and sent two knives cutting

their way through the rain and into the storming Freaks. One thrashed, a knife buried hilt deep in its chest. The other writhed, clutching at its stomach. Blood spilled, but it would live long enough to talk. Dodging a swing from a ham-sized fist, he ran from the advancing beasts. They turned and ran towards him, one of them limping behind.

"The kitten is sneaky," chuckled the one closest to him.

Gaining some distance, Deacon turned and more knives left his hands. He cursed as his fingers slipped on rain-slick steel. One blade grazed the side of a colossal face, leaving a gash. The other missed its mark and skittered away. Deacon drew the leather-handled blade from his back.

The wounded Freak dragged himself away from the fight. Deacon charged, running straight towards the nearing Brute. The big beast stopped and waited for him. Deacon smiled and leapt. Thick, crushing arms caught Deacon in a bear-hug and squeezed. Pain shot through his ribs as he thrust the knife into the creature's throat and sliced sideways. Blood spurted but the squeezing did not stop. Spots formed in his eyes as the wind left his lungs. He jabbed the blade repeatedly into the back of his captor's neck, hoping to sever its spinal cord. The limper neared. Deacon's victim crumpled to the ground, its grasp faltering as his arms fell open.

Deacon sprang free inhaling gulps of air. He dodged iron once again and rolled. The knife left his hand with a flick, the distance short and his aim true. A sick thud sounded as the blade hit its mark. The massive monster pitched face first onto the ground with a sigh as the life escaped his lungs.

He rolled the beast over and removed his knife from its blood-soaked eye socket.

The bleeding Freak was up the street, a rain-mixed blood trail oozing behind him. Deacon caught up with him, grabbed the creature's lank hair and snatched his head back.

"Where is Tyrant headed?"

Laughter.

His fist met the side of a greasy head. "I'm going to ask again. Where is Tyrant headed?"

More laughter. "Tell you nothin', nope, nothin', nothin', nothin'."

Deacon rolled him over and put his foot on its wounded stomach. The creature winced.

"If you don't tell me, I am going to cut your guts out and toss you over that fence to those dogs. Now, where is Tyrant headed?"

Tears streamed down a grimy face, as its eyes closed. Still he laughed. "What you lookin' for? Huh?" Rotted teeth showed as the creature grinned up at Deacon.

"Always the hard way. Fuck it." Deacon stepped on the creature's hand and pushed his blade into the soft cartilage of a jaundiced index knuckle. The creature screamed as Deacon removed its finger. He tossed the flesh over the fence.

Dogs snarled and fought.

"Dogs, you know, they don't kill. They eat their meat fresh and alive when possible. It takes a good while for you to die. But, if you answer my question, I'll finish you fast. Either way, death comes."

The Freak looked up at Deacon and glanced towards the fence and back to Deacon. "Tyrant south. South he said. Bring more to Ferrylinder, he said. What you lookin' for knife man?"

"A woman you took from up at Northhaven."

"Took lots o' women, Tyrant took 'em, took 'em to Ferrylinder," the creature grinned.

Deacon punched him again, "Dark hair, white dress."

"Oh her, you lookin' for the fighter?"

"Yes, the fighter," Deacon edged the knife into the crawlers jaw.

More laughter. "You won't find 'er."

"What do you mean, I won't find her?"

The Freak convulsed, coughed up blood and laughed more.

Deacon pushed the knife. "Tell me, or...the dogs..."

"That'un, a fighter. Uh, a fighter yah. She fought."

Deacon took a deep breath. "And?"

The crawler shook his head. "Would'n stop, see? Causin' trouble."

"Tell me!" Deacon yelled.

"Promise, knife man. Not the dogs, promise?"

"I promise," Deacon said through clenched teeth.

"She would'n stop screamin' and rakin' those nails. She 'scaped and ran. So big Unk, Unk he bopped 'er, see? Calm 'er down. But she don't move no more."

"Where?" Deacon's voice wavered as he asked.

Deacon's heart raced and his blood coursed hot.

A ragged yellow hand with a bloody stump pointed towards the cathedral. "By the bell, the big bell."

The blade came down again and again. Blood splattered, gore flew up, and it mattered not. What was once something almost human lay in the rain-soaked street, now a mass of blood and pieces.

Deacon made the slow walk to the old church as the rain washed chunks of red from his clothes.

There against a burnt wall lay his Sylvia. Blood stained her hands and tattered white dress. Lifeless eyes stared at him.

Deacon sank to his knees, took her cold hands into his as a wail escaped his throat and the Darkness came.

The sound of crackling fire roused his senses. Deacon peered through half-shut lids. He lay on a makeshift bed. Wood smoke and musk created a pungent bouquet in his mouth. Bare wooden walls with a few sparse pictures surrounded him. An old man sat on a rickety wooden stool, wearing overalls patched too many times and a faded flannel shirt. Lined with age, his face looked weary and his eyes held a certain sadness. He fed scraps of lumber into a fire.

"Damn near killed me getting you in here, way you were thrashing about." he said. "I know you're awake. You're safe here..."

Deacon sat up. "There is no such thing as *safe*."

"You did us no small favor killing them off. They were here for more."

"They took someone from me."

Cold reality sank in. She was gone and any joy he had known in this life was gone with her.

Rage filled him now. Rage at Tyrant, rage at the world he was born in.

Rage.

"They take from all of us, son."

"Yeah? What'd they take from you?" Deacon sneered.

The old man nudged the fire with a stick. Sparks flew up and the fire popped and snapped. He turned his head and looked at Deacon.

"Killed my son, took my daughter. Wife couldn't handle it, was too much..." the old man trailed off.

Deacon nodded. "I'm sorry."

The old man shook his head. "That was years ago. They come, take, and leave sadness behind. Thanks to you, none were taken today."

"That doesn't help me."

Deacon sniffed and cleared his throat.

"I know. We dug a grave for her. Was the least we could do."

"Show me."

Deacon eased out the door and followed the old man. The rain had stopped and the last rays of light broke through the departing clouds in the west.

"Name's Odell. Odell Hyde."

"Deacon."

Odell led him to a small church and then behind it. A cemetery sprawled before him. Tombstones from an age past. Crosses topped the heads of small mounds, along with various other monuments to the dead. A fresh grave lay open, Sylvia beside it laying in a slapdash wooden box. A ragtag group stood beside the grave, wet and somber.

"They're grateful, too. Figured you'd want to see her one last time."

"Thank you." Deacon looked at the ground. "I know you won't understand, but before we bury her, I have to do something."

His jaw clenched in bitter resolve. *Why?* Having to do this caused him more grief, but if others were to live he must do this last task. She would want him to. He was not sure he cared anymore. Without her, what was left of life for him? A lonely soulless world full of pain and sorrow. What joy he had known lay before him, no longer moving, no longer able to hold him, no longer able to speak the words his soul ached to hear one last time. His spirit belonged with her, traveling beyond the realms of death.

He would do this last duty for her because she would have asked of it him. Whatever feeling of belonging, of fitting in, of having a place that was his to be, was gone and he cared not for anyone nor anything left in Northhaven.

"Forgive me, my love," Deacon said as he knelt beside her and removed the knife from his back sheath.

His hand hovered over her lower stomach, over that other heartbeat that had also been stilled. All of their hopes lay cold and gone.

"Make them turn away," he whispered to Odell as tears slipped down his face.

"Turn around, please," the old man motioned with his hand at the group.

They obeyed.

With trembling hand, Deacon rested the knife's keen edge under her right eye and pushed.

He held a bloody cloth in his hands as he stood. This would be the last time she unlocked Haven. The cloth, with its cargo, he slipped into a pocket on his vest. He would need to hurry back to Northhaven. His grief would have to wait.

Deacon stood silent as they lowered her down into the cold black earth.

He took a clump of dirt and dropped it onto the makeshift coffin. Odell and some of the other men took their shovels and buried her. Deacon watched as piece by piece his humanity joined each clump of earth as it hit the wooden box.

He nodded his thanks to Odell and walked back to the corpses he had created. He felt nothing for them. The seeds of death had been sown. He would sow more before he was done. Deacon gathered up his knives, cleaned them best he could and walked back to The Hellion. He hit the power switch, entered his code and fired the bike up.

Standing outside of Northhaven, his last duty was complete. They had asked him to stay, but he could not. This place, it held too much pain for him now. It was ruined.

He had said his goodbyes and turned his back on Northhaven.

His father had been wrong.

The world could not be remade. What was left was despair, agony, and hatred. Hopelessness clouded his mind and rage filled his being.

A bright evening star shone in the night sky as he slipped on his jacket and cloaked himself in fury. Hellion's engine roared between his thighs. An oath he swore that day. An oath to avenge her. An oath to destroy Tyrant and his flesh trade. Then he would leave this place of sadness and join her.

Hell closed about him. The Darkness swirled on the outer edges of his consciousness and hatred drove him...south towards Ferrylinder.

Refuge of the Remnant
C.M. Bratton

Their eyes fill with mistrust. Underneath that, however, I spy the fear. The smell of it rolls into me, and only my full stomach keeps me under control.

That's how it always is now, when I venture out. No matter the IDs, no matter the controls, no matter the strict segregation, they still worry.

As they should. One day, their failsafes might stop working, and they will return to us once more. Until then, I live alongside them, doing their bidding, working for my keep, as it were. At least it's my choice.

"Get away, Remnant!" one of the guards spat as I drifted past on my way through the gate.

He was like most Normies – too big, too fat, too flushed with blood – for me to sympathize with.

Once, the Normies were on the run. Nearly gone. But everything changed after the Pulse.

Ten billion people on the planet. Then... the Infection. A billion died. Eight billion changed. A billion remained resistant. From their resistance the Pulse was born, and it reclaimed any who chose it.

We had adapted, we Pales. Eight billion of us, fighting for survival. Yet when the chance came to change back, to become a Normie once more, our numbers dwindled. From owning the planet for such a short time, we became a minority. The Remnant. Only a few hundred million left. Proud, too. We'd embraced our new heritage.

But the Resistants, the ones in power, were no longer concerned. We couldn't procreate, couldn't increase our numbers unless we shifted. And that had been strictly outlawed.

We were all provided a fresh supply of newly-deceased

brains as long as we stayed on our reservations and didn't shift. A few left to work for the government, as I did, but most of stayed on the res, just in case. Hard for a few to remain in control around all the fresh meat.

I'd been one of the first Pales, living in the city where it all started. The Infection mutated, as they do, and created various kinds of Pales. Some of us had more self-control, others less – and those were usually the ones with the younger strains of the Infection.

My life before... it wasn't worth fighting for. Lived in squalor in the slums of an overcrowded city. Volunteered for experiments not just for the money, but for a chance to be alone.

Guess I volunteered one too many times, but the way I looked at it, the Infection was coming one way or the other. I'd just had a little longer to get used to it.

It's probably why I applied to be a liaison between Normies and Pales. Resistants ran the planet, but they had no need to fear. We were allergic to them. We grew weak in their presence. We would never attack one, and that was how they taken the planet back.

Normies, on the other hand... it was hard not to sneer at the guard's fear, for it was a real one. Had I not been concerned for my own existence, I might have shifted and gone for him. In that state, bullets and Tasers didn't work. Nothing much did, except for Resistants.

But I had no desire for the guard. Or anyone, really. The brains delivered and served up were enough for me. As long as I stayed out of my shifted state, I stayed sane and in control.

And my people stayed safe.

I negotiated on their behalf daily. The government wanted to take away land on our reservations – never mind that with so many dead, there were plenty of resources available for all. The Resistants wanted to humiliate us, because we refused their Pulse. We liked who we were and what we'd become – our strength and unity and automatic support for each other.

I was the one who made sure they didn't lock us up on Greenland or some other hospitable place, but instead scattered reservations around the world. After all, we were just a remnant. We were only a danger in small doses.

In the end, we could be destroyed anytime.

But enough people who had changed from Normie to Pale and back sympathized with our decision. They fought for our rights, too.

I knew, though, that the Resistants were biding their time. All they had to do was threaten to take away the Pulse, and the Normies would all become Pales again.

And we'd starve.

I finally made it past the gate and into the reservation proper. The sky was darkening and I rushed to get back to the Central Facility where all our meetings took place. Many Pales lived there, including me, but there were just as many living in smaller homes dotted around the reservation. Becoming a Pale certainly hadn't made any of us kinder.

Still, tonight, we all gathered together for protection. Once a year, we closed the vaulted ceilings and sealed ourselves in. And then we waited, and hoped when we opened the walls up once more, we would still be safe.

There was a van that ferried us back and forth, and I managed to hop on before it left. The gate closed behind us, lights along the fencing turning red to show we were locked in.

Just as we wanted to be.

Pales were exceptionally talkative – shifting wore out the vocal cords. So the bus was quiet. There were only four others on it – not many would risk showing up late. Not this night.

The reservation was spread out, so the van drove along the single winding road for nearly a quarter of an hour before the trees widened and we arrived. There were several smaller, square buildings surrounding a huge, covered arena. All of the architecture was plain and functional, each place serving its purpose as a home or shop. Or in the case of the arena, a gathering place.

The government liked to think it knew our numbers. We were fitted with trackers, which alerted the Resistants if we shifted, as we occasionally had to. As long as we did that on the reservation, there were no repercussions, but any outside shifting was strictly regulated, buried under a lot of paperwork. Who wanted to shift like that? Shifting was power and reassurance. Our bodies repairing themselves. Our minds linking. It was heady and beautiful, but the Resistants wanted to make it profane.

The Normies knew. They had once been us, too. Their last shifts had been full of sorrow.

And many had regretted.

Hence, our growing numbers, albeit in secret. Normies who'd returned to diseased, crippled bodies found us in secret, trespassing against reservation boundaries and begging to return. All they needed to do was miss a Pulse, and the Infection would return.

If that was allowed.

But all Normies had signed an agreement to stay Normies. Any who violated that were sent to work camps for the rest of their lives. A different type of living death, so many chose to hide.

Here.

The van parked and we each hopped out. My own leap took me halfway across the lot and I forced myself to calm down. There was still enough time to get in and get settled.

The arena was another square, much larger than anything else, and rose four stories. It was open to the air, but it also had a retractable dome. The edges of it were beginning to rise. Once that was closed, the place would be locked down.

I entered and found the hallways empty. Everyone was already in place. I flashed my ID at one of the elevators and it opened up. I walked in and it closed behind me. The elevator went to only the top level.

The doors dinged and I stepped out. Here, finally, were a few others and I wound my way through the others until reaching my box. When I entered, a dozen others turned and met my gaze. Like me, they were some of the oldest Pales, products of the first generation of the Infection. The original strain. We were the most stable, so we made decisions on behalf of our people. Like me, they left the reservation and fought for our rights.

Like me, they waited for our return to power. For we didn't age and we didn't get sick. One day, however, the Resistants would, and so would the Normies. One day. We could wait.

I stared at them and they at me, but there was no need to speak. The edges of our thoughts reached for each other, and when we shifted, all would be known. And like me, they were worn out from a day of forcing themselves to speak to Normies at their speed. For now, our shared presence was enough.

In the meantime, I strode over to the viewing window. The arena was packed – nearly a hundred-thousand of us sitting quietly together. In the center, about fifty Normies stood, protected by a thick glass wall. They wanted to return, and this was their night to do so. But that first time shifting back was often chaotic, and they were caged for their own protection.

I looked up and found that the dome was more than three-quarters closed. Underneath it, a second dome was stretching out, made of titanium and lined with magnets. That was our real protection. Now that the Pulse was strong enough to send worldwide, we needed refuges like this one to stay safe.

The top layer closed, then the bottom. We were sealed in.

The lights changed, dimming to a pale blue. Speakers crackled. Nearby, one of the others hit the button that kept us connected with the other reservations. Yet another turned on the radio that tracked the outside world. The static continued for several long moments before a voice finally spoke, echoing into the arena with its eerie finality.

"The hour of the Pulse has arrived. The Resistant blood made into a wave that spreads its healing across the land starts now on the top of Mount Everest, the highest point in the world, re-built into a giant transmitter."

I tuned out the familiar story, instead thinking about the first time I'd encountered the Pulse. It was decades before, and the Resistants were only strong enough to build tiny transmitters. I'd been running towards a group of Normies, hunger spurring me on, when I'd seen several Pales drop. I'd been at the back of the crowd, which quickly cleared at they kept dropping, as boneless as if they'd been separated from their heads.

But we were in our shifted states. Unstoppable.

Then I saw them. A dozen Resistants holding a large machine that they pointed into the crowd. Whatever signal it was sending out, it dropped my fellow Pales in their tracks. They aimed it at me and I froze.

But either the signal was too weak or their power went out, for nothing happened. It was then I saw the others. They weren't dead, but writhing in agony. Color returned to their skin, flushing pink with the rush of fresh blood.

The scent invaded my mind, and I thought I might go mad with the hunger. They weren't Pales, but Normies.

Still, I was one of the oldest. I understood self-control and self-preservation. We couldn't win against a weapon we couldn't see, and none of us could attack a Resistant without growing weak. So I screamed a retreat. Most of the Pales with me listened, but many didn't.

They all became Normies and died.

"-that's... well, that's a bit unusual, folks."

The change in the narrative snapped me out of my reverie.

"The Pulse has increased its frequency... some sort of- of malfunction, it appears. Not to worry, though, because we are hearing from Resistant Central that it's just a glitch and the Pulse will continue as normal once it's fixed. Please bear with them. And indeed, our satellite feed shows a team of Resistants entering the device."

I exchanged glances with the others, tempted to shift and share our thoughts. But it was dangerous to shift during a Pulse, even with our protections. We could wait.

And wait. And wait.

The radio announcer and his hateful voice droned on, detailing the work the Resistants did as they repaired whatever faulty wiring was in their device.

"... and we are getting the thumbs up, everyone. The repairs are finished and the Pulse will resume. And there we are. It's begun. It's swept over Asia, and now Russia. Africa and Europe are completed, and it's sweeping across the Atlantic. There's North and South America, and finally, the Pacific. And done. There we are, folks, another year, another Pulse keeping us safe from the dead—uh, well. That's unprecedented. The Pulse is continuing for another round. Uh, that's, well, folks, let see if we've got any word from the ground... yes, it appears there's been a power surge. They're working on it now. Let's see, satellite feeds show- oh my God! No! NO! Oh shit. Shit, shit, shit! This is... it's gone. Everest is... gone. The device is gone. And the Pulse is... contracting, turning into a- a sphere or something."

Everyone glanced at each other uneasily, on the verge of shifting. But if we did, our hunger would return and we couldn't afford to waste supplies. Not with the Pulse floating around at random.

"The Pulse. It's not fading. It's just... moving along. It's down to about the size of Molokai, but it's still sweeping down the eastern Asian continent. I just... uh... shit."

His voice died.

I looked at the others and forced myself to speak.

"We must... keep all Pales... inside. Safe on the reservations. Until we... know more... no shifting. No leaving. We cannot risk the Pulse."

I looked down at the Pales below, their expressions frightened. The Pulse would destroy us all, and now it ran freely through the world. We could track it, at least, but for the moment, we couldn't move. Not yet. This was our refuge, and we couldn't risk losing ourselves.

Inside me, the hunger stirred. I hadn't shifted for a few days, and I might be able to go a few more. But there were a hundred-thousand of us in need of brains, and I didn't know when we could leave.

The Resistants couldn't let us starve. We'd shift and attack first. A lot of Normies would die. Too many. But with the Pulse out of their control, what next?

This thought preoccupied me for the following day. That was when the pounding began.

Someone – many someones – were outside the doors, trying to enter. I was hungry, barely in control, but I thought perhaps other Pales had come for help.

I staggered out and down the elevator until I reached the bottom floor. It was completely enclosed by metal and magnets, but there was a camera I could use to see outside. I walked to it, forcing my skin not to stretch, my teeth not to grow. There was time. I believed it.

I turned on the camera. Not a few, but thousands, stretching as far as the lens could see. Not Normies, but... Pales.

Not just any Pales. Near the front, I spied the familiar face of the gate guard, that had looked at me with so much hate a few days prior. They were all shifted, and their rage and hunger stripped away the last of my self-control. I let my walls dropped and changed.

The shift was rapid – one of my fastest ever – and I instantly felt their thoughts. I understood.

Their systems had been overloaded with the Pulse until it reactivated the Infection inside them, forcing them to change. All across the world, Normies were becoming Pales against their wills. But these Pales were mindless. All I sensed was hunger. A devastating hunger. If I let them in, they would devour us.

But... they were but recently shifted. Their brains were still fresh. A food supply, ready to go.

Satisfaction soaked into me and I disconnected from their minds. A new kind of Pale. One easy to trap. Easy to trick. Easy to eat. My claws flexed as I hissed in anticipation.

Then I screamed, a call to shift. A call to know. A hundred-thousand minds slammed into mine, and they knew. They understood. As one, we turned to the outside. First, satisfy our hunger. Then find out if the world was once again ours.

I hit the button to release the doors and in they flooded. We met them with joy. The first one I grabbed wore the face of the guard, a face I ripped off gleefully. As I finally sated my hunger, I realized that this boon was born of a two-sided coin.

Mindless Pales for us to feast on with their recently-dead Normie brains.

And a Pulse that could turn on any of us at any time.

As blood soaked the floor, I knew the world had changed yet again. We were no longer a remnant, perhaps. Perhaps even allowed to roam freely once more, away from the reservations.

But this place had been our refuge, and I wasn't going to leave it anytime soon. Not with the Pulse out there, the Resistants ready to crush us. For now, it was enough to satisfy the hunger and remember what I was meant to be.

INCIDENT AT KRAMER RIDGE
PATRICK NEAL

Acknowledgments:
I dedicate this story in part to my father Randy Cummings and to my mother Sandra Neal Cummings - thank you for the gift of life.

Chapter One:
Granddad's Map

"I'm a country boy at heart. Name's Vernon Grumlish, third generation tracker. Three generations have tamed this land, with even the same descendants of cattle we inherited down the line from the first settlers. In Kentucky, you tend to keep old traditions and take matters in your own hands. My grandfather Virgil always told his tale of his encounter with something he named 'The Man of The Woods.' I never believed him until years after his passing, I stumbled upon a map he drew in nineteen thirty-four to a place he nicknamed 'Squatch Holler.' It lies deep in the Appalachian Mountains, in the wooded area of the Catskill mountains."

The alarm went off and he looked at the clock. The red numbers piercing through the dark read 3:00 a.m. He hit the snooze button and fell back asleep. He tumbled through a dream rambling on about him living another life, sitting around a rectangular table with people he felt he knew. It seemed to be a few minutes, but turned into thirty as he woke up to the blaring alarm. He sprang from bed and quickly got dressed. He threw the basics into his bag: a multi-tool, magnesium firestarter, a flask of moonshine, and his survival knife, the handle of which was packed with fishhooks, waterproof matches, and water purifying tablets. He grabbed his grandfather's old compass and map, wrinkled in its old age. His friends Jeff and Taylor had already showed up and were sampling his breakfast when he came downstairs.

"Dude, hands off!" Vernon said as he swatted at his friends' grubby fingers.

He took the rest of his scrambled eggs and scarfed them down over the sink. He then reached for his OJ and noticed it already had both of their lip prints. He rotated the glass until no evidence of their mouths was on the rim and swallowed the rest.

"You text me when you get settled for camp," Matilda, Vernon's mom, said with a look of worry strewn across her face.

"Don't worry, he's in good hands with us," Jeff said.

"That's what I'm afraid of. If anything happens, then you boys just march on back here and I'll tan that old Bigfoot's hide!" Matilda said, turning on the oven.

"Okay mom, love you," Vernon said and kissed her cheek.

"Take the trash out with you. Be careful of the hillbillies and don't get shot wandering on their property!" she continued as she began to knead flour into dough on the counter.

"Yes, mom!" Jeff and Taylor said in unison, opening the screen door. Vernon gave the trash bag a spin and carried it out to the burn barrel and threw it in. He doused it with gas from an old rusty gas can and set it ablaze, emitting black smoke.

Jeff and Taylor held their breath rather than breathe in the toxic, sweet plastic smell as they hopped in Jeff's old Chevy pickup. He started her up and headed towards the highway. Lost Fork road jostled them around as they entered the ramp to I-75 North. A seemingly endless stretch of road beckoned them towards their destination as Jeff sped down the highway.

Parked behind a road sign of an enlarged map, a constable clocked the speed they were going. It read eighty-five mph on his radar gun. He threw on his sirens and sped up behind them.

"Dude, you're getting pulled over," Vernon said, seeing the red and blue flashing lights.

Jeff slowed the truck and pulled over on the shoulder of the highway. The constable parked behind them and got out wearing a tan uniform with the letters "J.L." sewn into his jacket.

He walked up to the driver's side window as Jeff rolled it down.

"What seems to be the trouble, officer?" Jeff asked, handing the officer his license and proof of insurance.

"I clocked you going eighty-five in a seventy-five mile an hour zone. What seems to be the hurry, boys?"

The constable looked in the window at Vernon in the backseat.

"We're on our way to the Catskill Mountains," Jeff said.

"Whatever for?" The constable asked, looking at his driver's license. His forehead wrinkled as he handed it back to Jeff.

"Oh, just some sight-seeing," Jeff said with a convincing smile.

"I'll let you off with a warning, but if I ever catch you speeding through my territory again, I won't be so nice. You boys have a good day," the constable said as he pocketed his pen and walked back to his car.

Jeff watched in the rearview mirror as the constable got in and drove off.

"Whew, that was a close one!" Taylor said, opening his hand. He was holding a spliff.

"Dude you didn't bring that with you, did you?" Jeff asked as he shifted the gear stick to drive.

The engine shook and sputtered as he sped up to sixty.

"It's just for hard times. I was gonna eat it if he wanted to search us," Taylor said, stuffing it in his flannel pocket.

Taylor and Vernon nodded off as small towns sprung up, neighboring endless fields as far as the eye could see. Jeff drove in silence, the way he liked it without all the chatter. That way he could listen to his old truck.

"She may be old, but she's got what it takes," Jeff said to his truck as if it were alive.

Time slipped by and Vernon nodded in and out of consciousness, seeing darkness begin to fall as they approached night. After driving six hours, Jeff pulled over at the rest stop, a junction between towns.

"Halfway there. We'll rest up here and leave at first light." Jeff said, parking in a spot between two trucks.

He leaned his seat back and pulled his hat over his face.

The three slept until something hit the window near Vernon.
      Startled, Vernon woke up and looked around in the still night. He saw the trucks were started up and tried to fall back asleep. He tried to get comfortable but couldn't, so he decided to get out and use the restroom. He walked to the bathrooms, but they were both locked. He walked behind the building where a barbwire fence was bordering a wooded area. He ducked underneath it and found a tree. As he relieved himself, he heard something rustling in the woods. He hurried up and turned to go back through the fence as the barbwire snagged on his pant leg. He tried to work it free, but heard a twig break and the crunching of leaves, like something was lurking in the dark. In a rush to get free, he tore his pants and cut himself on the rusty barbwire. He hurried back to the car and tried to open and close the door as gently as he could so not to disturb his friends. He locked the door and eyed the area, suspicious of any shadows that moved. He sighed and closed his eyes. Soon, he fell back into his light slumber.
      Hours later as dawn approached, the truckers went on to their destinations until they were the only ones left at the rest stop. The three of them all got out to take care of the morning duties and stretch their legs. A small van drove up and a man got out. He grabbed a bucket and a mop, then unlocked the bathroom doors for them. Vernon, who had woken up hours before, had already done his business so he waited for them. He looked at the tire tracks left by the trucks and noticed something sticking out of the dirt. He knelt and pulled it up out of the ground. It was a Bigfoot track on a key chain. He looped it on his key ring and pocketed it.
      Jeff came out of the restroom with a cigarette smoldering in his mouth. Taylor came out after him and they all shuffled back into the cramped car, crammed full of supplies for the trip.
      Feeling refreshed and the day renewed, they drove the final stretch towards the Catskill Mountains. Towns dotting the plain got more scarce as time drifted by faster than the day before. A feeling of excitement rushed through their stomachs as they drove past a sign reading, "Welcome to the Town of Catskill."
      "Vern, pop me one," Jeff said.

Vernon reached into a cooler they brought full of cold beer and ice. He grabbed one from the top and popped the tab. Jeff grabbed it, chugged, and threw the can out the window as he drove up to the Catskill Park entrance. They parked on the rocky lot in front of the trailhead and got out. They threw on their backpacks. Taylor picked up two water jugs tied to a PVC pipe and carried it like a yolk. Vernon and Jeff carried the cooler side by side as they ventured towards the campgrounds. Troops of javelinas marched through the campsite, searching for food left behind. Jeff kicked a rock to scare them and a javelina stopped in its tracks. It looked at him and snuffed, trotting off with its herd into the surrounding wilderness.

"Where do you want to camp? This place is crawling with pigs!" Taylor said in a harsh tone as the water jugs dangling from the crude yolk swayed in the wind.

"Primitive campground. Up just ahead," Jeff said, walking with his staff away from the RVs. They followed him to a trail sign marked, "Primitive Campground, camp at your own risk. Park not liable for any damages to vehicles."

Vernon looked at the sign and frowned, looking at Jeff and Taylor in question.

"Don't ask me, they probably referred to the legend," Jeff said as they tromped through the tall grass. The stopped in a circle of trees and all mutually agreed it was a good spot to set make camp.

Vernon had an A-frame instant tent that unfolded and popped open. He then hammered stakes into the rocky ground and secured his tent. He helped Taylor finish threading his tent poles and lashed them together as he staked it off. With the morning retreating and midday's sun high, they packed what they needed for the hike. Vernon checked his backpack, making sure he had the compass, granddad's map, a survival knife, and the firestarter. Jeff got his things ready. Instead of survival gear, he brought along his digital camera to capture evidence of the creature Vernon's granddad claimed to have encountered.

Securing their belongings in their tents, they set out for a hike to Giant Ledge, offering a scenic view of the Catskill Mountains. No hikers ventured beyond the park's border, but these were no ordinary hikers. Besides Vernon's dad and granddad being an expert tracker, his dad and Jeff's dad were best friends. Jeff was a second-generation tracker himself. Taylor usually tagged along with them, as the "Grunt", so they nicknamed him.

They passed the registration box and caught a breathtaking view of the Catskill Mountains from the first giant ledge. They continued in silence, rambling thoughts keeping them occupied as they hiked past all of the giant ledges overlooking an endless sea of trees, some turned rusty brown for that time of year. Panther Mountain stood alone, its peak covered in a cloud. They continued on to the Panther Mountain trail that led to the rolling Adirondack Mountains, looming there like sentinels overlooking the place for a timeless expanse. Jeff stopped at a rock to sit on and unzipped his backpack. He took out a trail cam and struck a match on the rock with his other hand, lighting a cigarette.

"You really need to stop smoking. It's a bad habit," Taylor said.

"Says the grunt who brought a spliff!" Jeff said as he handed the trail cam to him.

"Up there, Grunt. The trunk!" Jeff said, pointing to a hemlock tree.

Taylor climbed the Eastern Hemlock until he was standing on its pendulous branches. He positioned it high above his head, hanging it on a short branch.

"That'll do, good Grunt." Jeff said in approval.

"Will you stop calling me that? Damn!" Taylor said as he climbed down and a broken branch scratched him across his abdomen.

"Damn, that's gonna leave a mark!" Taylor said as he picked up his shirt, showing them the bloody scratch that started from his belly button all the way past his left nipple.

"When trees fight back!" Vernon said, chuckling. Taylor didn't think it was funny and fished in his backpack for his first-aid kit. They waited as he doctored his scratch with Band-Aids that barely hung on, losing their adhesive from the blood. He carefully covered it with his shirt.

"Tomorrow we come back, review the footage, and then we'll follow the map to Bigfoot Holler," Vernon said, turning back for camp.

They got there to find Jeff's tent was torn and ransacked. The other two were untouched. Jeff carefully inspected his tent, peeking inside. There was a bag of peanuts scattered in his tent.

"Damn javelinas!" Jeff said as he cleaned up the mess.

"We should hang our food out of reach of predators," Taylor suggested.

"Get a load of Grunt over here, expert at anything," Jeff said in a taunting manner.

Taylor mocked him and began to grunt as he gathered wood lying around their campground. He dropped it in a circle of stones, blackened from a previous campfire. He assembled them in a tepee like they showed him and was about to strike a match when Vernon said, "Woah!"

Taylor looked up at him as Vernon brought out his firestarter and survival knife. Taylor stood up and gestured with an open palm. Vernon shaved the magnesium into a dry bundle of dry grass. He cupped it in his hands and slowly blew it to life. Fire sprung from the smoldering coal and he set it under the kindling Taylor had gathered.

The firelight danced off the bark of the surrounding trees as the sun went down. The sounds of croaks and the rasp of locusts filled the night air as they sat around the fire, the flames licking the dark sky and crackling as they roasted hotdogs and ramen noodles and passed around a bag of pepper jerky.

Jeff grabbed a stick and stirred the coals, leaving it in to catch fire. The others waited anxiously for him to tell a story.

"And then there's the Legend of The Catskill Witch," Jeff finally drawled, knowing they loved hearing the tale, no matter how many times they heard it.

"The Legend of the Catskill Witch begins in ancient times around winter fires. The wise ones warned the warriors to take care when they went to the precipices of the mountains to hunt game, for they also might find a mischief maker, a trickster, an ancient woman who could take the form of a bear or a deer and lead the hunters astray, vanishing and assuming a terrible creature when they thought they captured her."

"How did she become this thing?" Taylor asked, stoking the fire as blue flames raced around the offering of a rotten log.

"An Indian witch who controlled the weather for the Hudson Valley, it was said she would reach up and pull pieces off from the moon, carve them into slivers and stars, and hang them in the sky," Jeff recounted from memory.

"That's old Indian Folklore," Taylor said.

There was a dead quiet, all except the crackle of the fire. Sitting across from him, Vernon gave a half smile.

"There's truth to every legend," Vern said.

"What about you, Vern? The story your granddad told you?" Jeff asked, leaning back on his elbows as the fire illuminated his face.

"It was in nineteen thirty-four, prohibition had ended but it was still the depression. My granddad had a younger brother and sister to take care of, his mother died from consumption, and his father, a railroad worker, was gone most of the time. He had to play the role of a parent and since there were no jobs to be had, he made a living doing the thing he was best at, tracking and trapping. They were poor, but he made sure they didn't go hungry. On a hunting trip, they ventured far into the Catskill Mountains, to a place he called Squatch Holler – the same place where we're going tomorrow. There, he and a friend had a standoff with a mother Bigfoot hiding a smaller one behind her. Then he was approached by the male. He said it was big, hairy, and manlike. He said the stench smelled like Satan's asshole. His friend shot at them and the forest people ran off. He drew this map of the place, the last thing I have of him," Vernon finished, clutching the folded map in reverence.

"We'll find out tomorrow. And we'll check the trail cam," Jeff said, before retreating into his tent and zipping it closed.

Taylor followed suit and also went to his tent for the night. Vernon sat up and watched the fire go out. He gazed up and saw the starry roof of the night sky, the light of countless unimaginably far stars twinkled. He laid back on the ground and closed his eyes for a moment. Among the chirps he heard a twig snap. He opened his eyes and picked his head up, looking around. Suddenly, something rustled the trees. He sat up and looked at the dark forest surrounding them. Another shuffle in the thicket behind him. He turned and suddenly something hard hit him on the shoulder. In the dying firelight, he saw a rock someone or something threw at him. He heard in the distance a knock that echoed through the valley. Then another knock in response from another location. The thought suddenly dawned on him as tingles radiated through the back of his neck.

They're here!

He remembered how his granddad would say they spoke back and forth to each other with tree knocks. To hear them doing it validated the story in his mind.

They were real.

That's why they are here, to prove the existence of Bigfoot, once and for all, he thought as he got into his tent. He zipped it closed and got into his sleeping bag, covering his head.

Bigfoot or not, I have to get some shut eye, he thought to himself as he dozed off from exhaustion.

Chapter Two:
Truths in Legends

The next morning, he was awoken by birds chirping and the sunshine poking through the seams of his tent. He unzipped the front and stepped out. There was a pot of coffee steaming away on the white ash-covered coals. Taylor was cooking eggs and Jeff walked out of the woods holding a roll of toilet paper.

"Something came through our camp last night. See? I don't think a bear did this," Jeremy said, showing him a cooler with a muddy hand print on the lid. "They took the lunch meat. We still have ketchup and mustard though!" he continued, trying to make light of the situation.

"I got this bruise last night from when a rock flew at my shoulder," Vernon said.

"Vern, that's just your imagination playing with ya." Jeff said jokingly.

"Well, rocks don't throw themselves," Vernon said.

"It could've been a ground squirrel, they get territorial," Taylor added.

"What a laugh. Do what you're best at, Grunt, and go fetch some water," Jeff said.

Without question, Taylor got the water bottles and went down to the stream, ebbing by his feet. In the quiet forest, he heard the trickle of the water and birds chirping as he filled each bottle. He stood up, slinging the homemade yolk carrying the water jugs over his shoulder and peered into the forest on the other side of the stream. Suddenly a tree moved. He did a double take and stared quietly into the forest for it to move again. He diverted his eyes as he rotated, he saw something brown dash out of the corner of his eye. He quickly looked all around and again saw nothing. He hurriedly carried the water back to camp.

Vernon avoided talking about the night before and kept to himself as he filled his water bottles and dropped a water purification tablet in each. They shared breakfast consisting of bacon and eggs cooked in a paper bag before securing their tents. Then they set off for Squatch Holler.

The sun winked through the canopy high above them, taking its place in the morning sky. Vernon reached in his backpack and fished out the map and compass. He carefully unfolded the map nearly a century old and held it out in front of him. He compared it to the tops of the mountains in the distance and they lined up. They followed the trails to a wooden sign reading "Devil's Path." They followed it towards a dried-up riverbed, using the map to guide them.

On the map, it showed a ridge near the foot of a mountain. Excitement welled up inside them with the thrill of adventure as they followed the creek bed to nowhere, surrounded by the forested expanse.

"What do you think your family will think when we bag Bigfoot?" Jeff asked, stepping past the loose stones in the riverbed.

"We won't bag him as you so eloquently put, just try to prove it's real," Vernon said, kicking a stone in front of them.

"You always take everything so serious, Vern. I meant video," Jeff said, holding his digital camera, taking snapshots of Vern giving him the finger and their hike through the dry creek.

Upon walking around a bend in the creek bed, they startled something in the nearby bushes. Jeff, Vernon and Jeremy's eyes picked up on the movement of the animal in the dense woods, running low to the ground like it was something other than a deer. They looked hard as Jeff took video of the surrounding wilderness. Whatever it was, was gone now.

At the end of the dry creek, they faced an impasse, a rocky ridge running along the foot of Westkill Mountain, written in blue pen ink on the map as 'Kramer Ridge.' Jeff eyed the map as he walked side by side Vernon.

"I'm glad we got this opportunity, man," Jeff said as Taylor, acting as the scout, inspected the rocky ridge that rose two stories into the air. The only way to go was along it. One by one, they scaled the ridge, walking sideways along its smooth surface as they slowly ascended. At the end of the ridge was a forest at the base of the mountain. Vernon looked at the map and wondered why this mountain was called Westkill in the first place as he jumped off the ridge, into the forest. The other two followed, Jeff with his camera capturing video of everything as he walked.

Vernon's heart raced. He knew this was Squatch Holler, as written on the map. He carefully stepped over the fallen tree limbs, trying not to break them and alert anything of their presence.

"Woo check this out!" Jeff said, standing in front of a large sapling that had been broken over at the top, several feet above their heads.

"Wonder what could do that?" Taylor asked as he pointed at another large sapling, broken in the same fashion.

Vernon's heart pounded as he realized the strength of something that could snap a sapling like a twig. A deep thud resounded from not too far off. They froze as they waited in silence. Then another thud, this time it sounded closer. Jeff, oblivious of the danger, kept shooting with his digital cam. Vernon stopped and looked into the dense wilderness of branches laced in front of him.

Something in the dense woods snorted and snuffed. To Jeff, it sounded a lot like a deer in rut. They curiously ventured further into the forgotten forest where the noise was coming from and suddenly Vernon heard something behind him whisper something, followed by a chirp. He turned around quickly and something furry darted behind a tree. He looked at Jeff and pointed in the direction behind them.

"*Cacow!*" A shrill voice sounded from all around them, echoing off the trees.

Taylor brandished a sharpened shank wrapped with electrical tape for the handle, holding it ready for anything to come out of the woods.

Vernon stopped and heard rustling behind him again, then it ceased. He took another step and heard another shuffle of leaves. He kept walking, knowing something was following them. Jeff walked over to a tree structure woven together at the top and sides. Vernon walked over to the structure looking at it in awe, realizing he was stepping foot on the same turf granddad did so many years ago. He saw a woven entrance to the structure and ducked to look inside. He saw there were smaller sticks woven into a nest. He sniffed and it smelled like wet dog on a summer day and baked up as Jeff made sure to follow up with his camera.

An inhuman yell broke the silence. They looked around, Jeff sweeping the area with his camera. Vernon kept his eyes straight, looking the direction of the yell. Suddenly something hairy walked from behind a tree and then went behind another.

"Guys!" Vernon said sternly and motioned with his eyes.

They looked in the direction where he was staring and some of what they thought were trees began to move, stepping out from hiding for them to see. They were big as trees, some even wearing pieces of tree bark to conceal themselves. Vernon picked out a mother shielding two adolescents with large black eyes that were almost their height, at least half the size of the ones standing shoulder to treetop.

Jeff continued to take video of the sasquatches that revealed themselves to them. Vernon reached in his backpack and offered them stale crackers, setting it on a stump. Taylor suddenly lunged at them and the tribe of sasquatch disappeared once again, all except one that stood head and shoulders above them, about nine feet tall. It was reddish brown, with long gray whiskers on its manlike face. It picked up a large tree branch in front of it and hurled it at them, Taylor narrowly dodged it as it crashed into a tree above him. It then growled in an earth-shaking tone, charging at them, reaching for Jeff's camera. It grabbed him by the shoulder and took the camera. It pushed him far into the trunk of a tree, knocking him almost unconscious. The beast toyed with the camera for a moment, seeing its reflection in the lens, and then let out a low gurgle as it knelt and smashed it into pieces on the ground. Seeing it was destroyed, it curiously looked at them, eyeing Vernon as Jeff looked at it in awe. Taylor, afraid, didn't make eye contact with the beast as it felt his hat and took his backpack. It walked away, keeping its souvenir as it disappeared into the forest.

Vernon stared into the woods until the trees no longer moved. They all mutually agreed without words to head back to the trail. Upon venturing back to the ridge, Vernon spied out of his peripheral a pile of bones. He went to look and recognized a femur. The others noticed what he was looking at and stood next to him. In the pile of bones, they saw bits of wallets and car keys, torn jeans, and flannel. Vernon noticed there were teeth marks on the bones, nearly stripped of flesh.

Suddenly it donned on him that this wasn't a Bigfoot graveyard, but a feeding ground. He ran towards the ridge and began to scale down, nearly slipping as a sasquatch leaped at him from hiding in the rocks below. It clawed at his feet as he made his way across. Jeff also scaled the ridge, nervously looking down and seeing the scattered bones and souvenirs of unfortunate campers as he made his way down to the dry creek.

Vernon, last in line, shimmed across the ridge when a hairy hand reached over the top of the ridge and grabbed his left hand. He struggled against the beast, yanking his hand free as he lost his footing and fell off the ridge, landing on one foot and rolled his ankle. He grabbed his ankle as he felt the pain shooting and radiating up his leg. He tried to stand, but couldn't bear weight due to the extreme pain.

"Go get help, I'll just slow you down!" Vernon said, accepting his fate, as he saw two sasquatches clear the ridge in a blur, cutting off Taylor and Jeff's escape route. The sasquatches growled as they slowly stepped towards them, bearing their teeth with a crazed manlike expression written on their faces covered in hair.

Vernon forced himself up to stand, using the ridge to help him. He hopped on his good foot and leaned back against the ridge. He felt with his hands engravings in the rock. He looked down and saw along the base of the ridge were petroglyphs carved into it, depicting men with spears attacking hairy manlike beasts and an anomalous figure that had a crown fashioned from sticks. He gasped and looked straight at the two sasquatches, standing twice as tall as all and closing in and cornering them against the ridge. Vernon stared at something in the woods, he thought he was hallucinating as he watched branches twist and form into the shape of a deer.

"Well, it looks like we proved the existence of Bigfoot!" Taylor said with morbid sarcasm, shaking to the core as one of them let out a guttural growl and charged him, grabbing him by the throat and pinning him against the rock. The sasquatch studied him with big black eyes obscured by its bushy eyebrows.

Suddenly, what they thought was a tree next to the ridge moved. It turned around and before them stood an even larger sasquatch, head and shoulders above the others, its fur resembling tree bark. It leaned forward to look at them inquisitively. The map fell out of Vernon's pocket. He reached to grab it and almost lost his footing. The patriarch swiftly stepped up and grabbed the map with its large forefinger and opposable thumb and sniffed it. Jeff sat with a face of frozen terror as one of the sasquatch sniffed his shirt.

Vernon stood, looking up at the giant manlike beast examining the map. Out of the corners of his eyes on both sides, he saw other sasquatch emerging from the woods, curiously watching them with black soulless eyes.

Something else emerged from the woods, a large deer with branchlike horns. It stamped its foot and exhaled steam through its nose, eyeing the sasquatches. The sasquatches gave the large buck a wide berth as it inspected them.

"Please don't hurt us, we have food!" Jeff said, offering a pack of jerky. The sasquatch took the bag of jerky and reached in and took out the freshness packet and stuck it in its mouth and gnashed it with its huge molars.

"No, you don't want to eat that!" Jeff said.

The sasquatch spit the packet out as the deer snuffed, turned, and trotted off into the dark forest. Vernon watched it walk away and its leg became a snake that slithered off into the forest, its horns became branches and its body became a dead tree trunk covered in mushrooms.

Towering above them, the largest sasquatch growled and Vernon felt the vibration resonate through the rock behind him. He slowly backed away from the three sasquatches, seemingly deciding what to do with them.

Vernon limped as Jeff caught him, helping him stand. The patriarch watched them and turned his attention to Taylor, reaching out and wrapping his long fingers around one of his legs and carried him upside down, stepping up the ridge. Taylor's world turned upside down, he looked down and saw behind the ridge, piles of bones and more souvenirs and torn clothing. Blood rushed to his head, now turning beat red in the sun. He felt sleepy and began to black out as just as the largest sasquatch dropped him on a pile of bones.

He sluggishly reoriented himself by sitting up, looking up at the long, trunk-like legs of the sasquatch stepping over him and reaching down for Jeff. In one hand, the largest sasquatch grabbed Jeff and began to squeeze.

Jeff felt his rib cage crack as he fought for breath. The other sasquatches began to inspect Taylor's clothes, taking his personal belongings. First it was his watch, then one of them found a gun. They began to fumble with it. The patriarch saw it and lunged forward as the gun went off, wounding the one holding it. It let out a yell and ran off into the woods.

Jeff gave chase, firing into the woods at the fleeing sasquatch, darting from tree to tree like a shadow. He followed its trail of blood droplets and got excited, thinking he had wounded this thing and he had the upper hand. Just over a hill, he approached the wounded sasquatch cowering at the base of a tree, clutching its face with black fingers and reddish-brown fur. Jeff cocked the gun and aimed at it. It then moved its hands and he hesitated for a timeless moment, looking at this thing that looked almost human. The sasquatch let out a low whimper, almost asking to be spared. Jeff lowered the pistol, feeling sorry for this thing and turned his back on it, walking away.

As he walked away, the sasquatch rose up behind him. Its shadow crept up the bark of the tree and its bones snapped as its fur rippled and it began to change shape. It morphed into a giant sloth, bear-like creature with ten inch claws and spiky horns branching from its head.

Jeff heard the scuffling and stopped. He turned around quickly and saw the huge beast standing there, towering above him, breathing heavy with its salivating mouth agape. It let out a gurgling roar and Jeff caught wind of its putrid breath.

He fired at the creature and ran away from it as it crashed through the woods after him, breaking branches in its path like they were sticks. He ran back to Kramer Ridge and saw the largest sasquatch and the other one standing in front of Taylor and Vernon, as if protecting them from this thing. Jeff stopped and looked around, aiming the pistol in a dizzy circle at nothing.

In his moment of recovery, the forest stopped spinning around him as branches and leaves began to twist behind him and the creature reappeared, more menacing before with an elongated mouth and two rows of sharp teeth. The patriarch tore a sapling out of the ground and threw it like a spear at the creature. It caught the sapling in its jaws and bit it in half, snapping it like a twig.

More terrified than amazed, Vernon watched from behind the ridge to see the largest sasquatch seemed to be protecting them. This Patriarch let out a high-pitched squall and the woods around them began to shake. Sasquatch calls began to sound all around them from the nearby mountains. The creature wailed as Jeff climbed the ridge where he and Vernon watched it retreat into the forest as its leg detached and became a snake that slithered off into the leaf litter, its horns wove into branches of a tree above it, and its torso became a fallen tree trunk covered in mushrooms.

Vernon crawled down from the kill site, baffled and mystified. He picked up the gun and lifted it, getting the large sasquatch in his sights. He felt for the trigger and aimed at the giant sasquatch's face, now with a familiar expression of despair. He lowered the pistol and the giant sasquatch hesitated for a timeless moment, gazing at him with his black human-like eyes, then turned and slowly walked away, quietly retreating back into the forest.

Taylor and Jeff walked out of there on either side of Vernon, helping him walk out of the dry creek that led them there. Vernon looked back and saw the map laying where the sasquatch had dropped it.

"What is it?" Jeff asked.

"Nothing. Let's go," Vernon said, leaving the map behind, the only thing that could prove the existence of sasquatch.

"We should call the police!" Taylor said as he checked an old phone booth, listening for a dial tone.

He dialed 911 on the rotary phone and soon the park police arrived.

One by one, they told their story of the incident at Kramer Ridge. The police scoured the area, finding no signs of the sasquatches, of the bones and souvenirs that had somehow disappeared. The detective on the scene figured it was another Bigfoot hoax when he saw in the mud a wedding ring sticking out of the ground. He reached down to pick it up, feeling it was stuck to something. He yanked harder and a finger came loose from the soil, still attached to the ring.   --The End

NO. 14
KEVIN LOONEY

> "Apollo may be the God of Sculpture. But in the extreme he is also the God of Light and in the burst of splendor not only is all illumined but as it gains in intensity all is also wiped out. That is the secret which I use to contain the Dionysian in a burst of light."
> -Mark Rothko, No. 14 (Painting), 1961, Oil on canvas, the Houston Museum of Art.

As I gaze upon its simple yet elegant magnificence, I wonder how some could dare to question Rothko's genius. Some of my friends have referred to his work as childish. One even went so far as to have his four-year-old daughter try to duplicate some of his canvases on an eight-and-a-half-by-eleven piece of paper. The idea of shrinking his grand work down to such a small size with Crayola watercolors is one of the most absurd concepts I've ever encountered. I mean, sure, her rectangles were pretty good, but they lacked emotional depth. They lacked the touch of the divine.

That's right. I said it — my most absurd theory. Mark Rothko, while not a god himself, worked alongside them. Well, not so much *them*, but one in particular: Apollo. The Greek celestial was known as a god of many things, but what concerns my theory the most is his dominion over the arts and light. He imbued Rothko with his power, or perhaps Rothko found a way to take it by force. I don't have all the answers, but I suspect the art curators at the Houston Museum of Art have also suspected what I believe to be true. Otherwise, why choose to put the quote they did on the placard next to the giant No. 14 I'm staring at?

Rothko was obsessed with the mythological and spiritual and how it connected to art, emotion, and the human experience. He was also a follower of the philosophical teachings of Nietzsche who was in turn fascinated with all things Apollonian and Dionysian—terms he used relentlessly. It's clearly linked, but in a way few have deduced.

Which is why – finally – it is time for me to finish the investigation of my theory. I need to touch the painting, but the museum worker — or guard, if you want to call him that — refuses to leave. It feels like his eyes are focused solely on me. He looks to be about fifty or so, and if I had to guess, he is probably close enough to six-foot tall that he rounds up whenever someone asks because it sounds better than saying five-eleven-and-a-half. The man has the physical build of someone who was in shape during his prime but has long let himself go in favor of a reclining chair and fried food. This is probably the only exercise he gets anymore, pacing along the brown hardwood floor.

Most of the time, he walks back and forth in front of some blue, green, and yellow blob that is attached to a freestanding wall on the far end of the room near to an entryway. Blob: that's what I call that form of abstract art. I'm not familiar with the artist. I know it isn't a Pollock as it is more stroke than splatter, plus there is an actual Pollock here on the wall behind me, and it looks nothing like that thing. I can certainly see value in the work, but it is too chaotic for my personal tastes.

It isn't the large canvas that bothers me, though. It is the person crowding it. Every time I think he's going to walk around to the back side of the wall, instead he stops, looks at me, and turns back around. I don't know how, but he must be on to me. There are at least a dozen other patrons in the spacious room, but none of them seem to draw his attention. While I could get at least one finger to make contact before getting tackled, I need to do far more than that to complete my investigation. Fortunately, I have concocted a plan.

During one of my previous visits, I took a video that was truly revealing. I saw... well — something akin to what one might capture in a haunted house video. I used to go on ghost hunts as a teenager before I refined my fascination with the supernatural toward the divine. Sometimes, I would catch flying orbs in the video footage, and once, I even heard an odd whispered plea at the same time one of those balls of light zoomed by. It said, "Tell Michelle to bring me a beer. You can take things with you when you die."

Of course, at the time, I had no idea who Michelle was,

but I later did a little research and discovered she was the eighty-year-old widow of the guy who used to live there. He'd been dead thirty years. She never remarried. I managed to track her down and show her the footage. From what I heard, she returned to the house the next day and died there that night with a bottle in her hand, which had to suck for whoever owned the place. And while this is an important illustration that I swear has a point, I'm getting a little off-track.

After I saw the light in the video I took of Rothko's painting, I was knocked unconscious for about seven minutes, though it felt like much longer. I heard a voice repeatedly say "free me" while I was out. The extra weird part was that the voice sounded similar to what I've heard from Rothko from a YouTube clip. I don't think the artist is trapped in the painting, but perhaps Apollo's manifestation somehow merged with Rothko's essence. Art can hold more than a mere shadow of the divine.

Now, back to the security guard and how all this connects with the video footage. It took some exploring of the dark web — thank goodness for VPNs — but eventually I found a guy able and willing to hack the cameras of the museum. I had a very specific request, one which I wasn't sure was even possible, but he assured me he could make it happen for some Bitcoin. Luckily, I invested early in cryptocurrency.

My request: feed the footage that knocked me out into the museum's system to project that image outward, so it fills every room of the museum. Yeah, my idea sounded like some heist movie make-believe Hollywood hijinks, and I thought it was until the guy said it was doable. Sure, I believed he was likely just telling me what I wanted to hear to milk me for more money, but it was hard to say. I must solve this mystery even if I end up bankrupted by this internet swindler. I'm willing to give it a go.

I glance down at my watch. Five more minutes. Don't look at the camera. Don't look at the camera. While it isn't like that ten-dollar-an-hour security guard has any inkling about the reality of my plan or could conceivably stop the already turning wheel, it would be best to minimize my trail of breadcrumbs.

If everything goes according to plan — if I am right — I will soon be meeting a god. I glance down at my feet. I'm wearing ratty, decade old tennis shoes, ripped jeans, and an oversized t-shirt with a comic book character plastered across the front. My efforts to look like an average joe may be successful, but is this how I want to appear to the god of light? I mean, at least he isn't the god of fashion sense, right?

I shake my head and move my gaze away from my laces and back to the painting. Soon, this masterpiece will be destroyed thanks to me. It is not only important, but vital for the art community that I absorb the beauty of this thing one final time. Of course, it was nearly impossible for me to admire its grandiose beauty without incorporating my theories of majestic intervention.

I focus on the largest shape, the brown rectangle that consumes about two-thirds of the paining. The edges of it, specifically along the bottom and the right side, are lined with a thin, jagged stripe that is a lighter shade. All three of the rectangles do this to some degree, but while the top section reminds me of a dirty sun mixed with mud and blood and the bottom looks like a nearly non-existent creeping shadow of that, the middle forces the truth of mathematics into my right-sided-brain-focused self.

Ninety degrees. That's what I see. Those two lighter brown lines make me think of geometry. In high school, I was an A+ art student, but a C- math kind of guy. Sometimes the two seemingly disparate worlds intertwine, and no one knew that better than Rothko. In the case of the No. 14, I believe there was an even more focused intent. I may not have retained much from tenth grade geometry, but I remember my teacher drawing a dotted line angled diagonally from the corner where the two lines intersected. If my theory proves to be right, and I pray to whatever deity may be listening that I am, then I must make these imaginary lines real.

I glance at my wrist again. The minute hand is one tick away from hitting the twelve while the red one marking the seconds approaches the three. Only forty-five seconds to go.

Breathe, man, breathe. I've got this.

I rub my hands together like a classic mustache-twirling villain growing antsy while his plan approaches the point of fruition. Perhaps it is my paranoia kicking in, but I look back over where the guard has been positioned during my entire time in this room. Strangely, he is no longer there. I furrow my brow. Now? He chooses now to move.

And I feel it—like a kid who knows he's done something wrong and can sense the eyes of a parent baring down upon him. Less than a minute left, and now he pulls this ridiculous maneuver. Whatever. It's too late. It doesn't matter. Or, at least it won't if my hacker friend is successful.

I turn around to see him staring right at me.

"Hey," I say, stretching the word out long enough to eat up an additional second.

He stares at my eyes. "Weird contacts."

He's right. They are, but I don't care how weird they look as long as they work. I bought some reflective mirror lenses at a cosplay shop that are similar to what Vin Diesel wore in *Pitch Black*. My hacker friend assured me they should block out the image from penetrating my brain, though he did recommend I still try to close my eyes the moment the image projects. "Thanks?" is all I say.

He smirks, then leans in a closely and whispers, "I want in."

My eyes dart around the room. This is not what I expected.

"Excuse me?"

"You're clearly planning something. I've been watching you come in and stare at this painting for weeks now. Sometimes, you even take photos or video of not just it, but the whole room. You're clearly planning to steal it, and I... want... in."

Wow. This is not at all how I pictured this encounter going, despite the numerous scenarios I've played out in my head. So, I give him the stupidest, most cliché, paper-thin response I could conceive in the moment.

"I'm sorry, but I think you're confusing me with someone else."

He tilts his head to the side and stares at me with that classic "I'm not falling for that trick" look. I glance again at my watch. Five seconds.

Four.

Three.

A flash happens.

He opens his mouth like he's about to say something, but instead collapses to the floor. Luckily for him, his head lands against his arms and not the wood.

Hmmm... a couple seconds off. I guess my watch isn't fully calibrated. My eyes weren't closed, so good to know the lenses work. Groovy. I don't think Diesel would say that.

All right, I don't have long — just a mere seven minutes — assuming the video has the same effect on everyone else that it did on me. I look around. The others in the room and those I can spot in the nearby connecting hallway have gone unconscious. Perfect.

Before I can continue to the next step, I need something else. Multiple somethings. I run quickly back to one of the rooms I passed through on my way here, careful not to step on anyone as I go. There are ancient works of art in here like a portrait of the Roman Emperor Caligula in bronze. These are all positioned on stands with clear plastic boxes encasing them. I take down four of the boxes, which is the most I can carry in one trip and return to the No. 14 as fast as I possibly can, setting the boxes next to me. I don't need them yet, but I will soon. Hopefully, they'll hold my weight. I figure if airplanes can use acrylic plastic for their windows and we don't all die as a result, these should be able to hold my scrawny body.

I pull out my pocketknife, flip it open, and take a deep breath. I've got this. But before I act, I need to do one last thing. I run my fingers along the surface of the painting, and my whole-body tingles. It doesn't feel quite like electricity, but I don't know how else to describe it. It's like how I felt once when a ghost passed through my body but spread equally across every square inch of my skin. I must be right.

I hold up the knife to the bottom right corner of the middle rectangle. I make a small incision—about one inch in length—and wince. *It's okay. You're not destroying a great piece of modern art*, I tell myself. *You're helping an ancient deity that's probably going to be grateful when you free him.*

I keep going, careful to keep my dotted line mostly straight. That's part of the key: perfection within the subtle imperfection. When I can no longer reach, I move the plastic boxes into place. They creak as I step onto them but seem to hold. Thank goodness. I finish the last line, careful to not cut past the top left corner of the rectangle. Not done yet. The last part will take some stretching even with the extra height. Luckily, I'm on the tall side and have freakishly long arms.

The top dirty blood rectangle must be cut out entirely. Well, almost entirely. I plan to leave a ninety-degree set of lines from the point where I just stopped along the left side and the top. I know this whole process sounds like wild conjecture, but while I was unconscious, I saw strange images that didn't make much sense at the time, but the more hours I stared at this painting, the puzzle pieces started to connect.

I glance down at my watch and realize everyone will wake up in about the next three minutes. I really should have made sure to take my Adderall this morning.

Focus and finish this thing. And that's exactly what I do, though it takes me nearly two minutes. That's okay. There is just one more step that needs completed. I get down from atop the boxes, then take one and turn it to where the open end is now facing me. I stuff the cut canvas inside it, pull out a small flask, and dash some vodka on top of it before removing a lighter from a separate pocket. A few seconds later, flames start to consume the cut fragment. I don't let it go for too long before I stomp my boot covered foot inside the box to extinguish the flame. The plastic didn't melt yet—once again proving its strength.

Fifteen seconds left...

I grab some ashes and smear them on the bottom rectangle and then take a few steps back and stare. The once magnificent work of art is destroyed. Please let my heinous act mean something. C'mon.

Ten seconds...

A white light forms around the frame of the painting and shoots out, forcing me to close my eyes, but even with them shut, I still see it. And then, just like that, my body collapses as I descend from light into darkness.

An instant later, I'm standing alone in a white room. No, I'm not alone. A man stands before me whose face does bear some resemblance to Rothko, though that's where the similarities end. He has blonde hair with red tips and is dressed like a punk rocker. Suddenly, I don't feel so self-conscious in my old clothes.

"Thanks. Took long enough."

I simply stare.

"And now is that pivotal moment in the script when you say you're welcome."

"I... yes, of course," I stutter, making a fool out of myself before a god. "You're welcome."

"There you go, that's better."

I smile. "I apologize for having to ask, but... are you Apollo?"

"That's a big, fat N-O."

A giant bottle of wine appears in his hand. He waves his fingers above it and the cork pops out. He catches it mid-air, brings it to his nose, and smells it before throwing it back over his shoulder. He takes a swig, then stretches out his free hand and introduces himself.

"Dionysus."

Not sure how to react, but not wanting to insult him, I shake his hand. "But the quote said Apollo, plus all the clues pointed toward him. I mean, Rothko was an artist."

Was that a bark-laugh I just heard, or did he choke on the wine?

"Well, he shared some of my passions as well." He takes another generous swig. "But I can see how 'I used to contain the Dionysian' is so confusing."

Was he mocking me now?

"If it makes you feel better, I fooled him into trapping Apollo elsewhere. He thought it was me, but well..." He bows dramatically with his arms flung outwards. "I drove him more and more towards wine. He eventually caught me off-guard while I entertained a trio of models."

He stares off, smiling.

"Yeah, that night alone was definitely worth a few decades of imprisonment. For me, I mean. There's that whole immortal god thing. Besides, my bottles kept him company while I was gone."

"Yeah, sure, until he killed himself less than ten years after making this painting."

"Well, I can't take all the credit for that. Man is inherently weak and obsessive. Enough chit-chat. Time to get out of here."

He takes a few steps backwards and looks me up and down.

"Now, I need you to not move. Okay?"

"What?"

He snaps his fingers, and I feel my feet sink into the ground. I try to lift them, but it's useless. The white walls around me morph into connected images of the painting I just destroyed. It then spreads to the ceiling and the floor.

He winks at me and then vanishes — wine bottle and all. I see an image appear in the middle rectangle of the paintings. It is Dionysus offering his hand to help up a middle-aged security guard from of the floor of the museum. Afterwards, he turns and looks at me through the resurrected painting I had destroyed. Reflected in his eyes, I see it there unharmed, the No. 14 — my new home.

BEHIND THESE EYES
C.M. BRATTON

    Did they ever look up and really expect to see us when we dropped down in our ships, the clouds boiling away from the heat of our engines?
    Did they know it was time for their end?
    When did they realize they were dying? Did any of them wonder if we had a choice? Could we have passed them by, living securely in their luminous blue sphere shining alone in the empty waste of their galaxy?
    And the survivors. What makes them so defiant, still, so full of the belief that there is a reason to keep living, keep trying, keep defying their captors? We have no words in our language for this useless emotion, what they call "hope." Don't they understand that they've already lost, as we nearly did, until we learned to be as hard and cold as our conquerors? Until we forgot remorse and compassion, decisively annihilating those hated ideals from our very DNA in favor of survival at any cost?
    Including the destruction of an entire world, of millions of species, of another sentient life form – a rarity in this expanding and mostly dead universe.
    Do they know we destroy their world to keep ours alive?

    I stopped reading and took a deep breath, my heart pounding away inside my chest. I looked back down and stared at the transcription, interspersed under the translation I could see unfolding behind my eyes. How I could read and understand it, I didn't know. But more importantly, I didn't know why it had been given to me.
    Cars rolled past me, oblivious as I sat on the park bench. The sky above was tranquil and pale blue, the grass waving gently in the spring wind. A perfect day, I'd thought.
    I rubbed my eyes, trying to erase the words printed there. Did I hold a history – or a prediction?

Unable to take "reading" any more of the alien script, I rolled it up into a diminutive cylinder and slid it back in its case, which looked like a cross between a cigar holder and a leather case for glasses. Only instead of leather, it was made out of some metallic material that caught and reflected light in such a way as to make the object mostly invisible to ordinary vision. I closed my eyes and leaned back, replaying the pictures of last night in my mind in an effort to erase the indigo script flowing behind my eyelids.

I'd been woken up just a few hours before dawn. My stomach was clenched in a tight knot and there had been a pressure banding my head, more tightly than any migraine I'd ever experienced. I opened my eyes at that point, but was unable to see the dim light that usually filtered through the curtains of my window.

Palms sweaty, I made as if to get up, but a voice I felt more than heard said, "Shh."

I froze, my body breaking out into goose bumps even as my lungs froze. A moment of heart pounding terror passed, then suddenly, it was gone. The pressure left and the room brightened again. The outline of the window reappeared. I shakily managed to sit up, but as I started to move my hand, a shock of cold fire blazed in my palm. I let out a small shriek of pain and clutched my hand to my chest, but even as I did, the burn faded to a cool ache. As I unclenched my fist, I felt the shape of a cold cylinder just longer than my hand and half as wide. I tried to see it in the dim light, but only its slight weight was discernible.

I'd lit every light in my little apartment and spent the rest of the early morning either pacing or staring at the thing I'd left sitting in the center of my bed, as if peering at it would make it easier to see or explain its presence.

By late morning, the sun streaming through the edges of the curtain, I'd made no decisions, so I'd decided to come to the park and go for a jog to clear my head. But before I could so much as start stretching, I'd felt a cold burn flash momentarily in my hand. It was immediately followed by a cylindrical shape, my hand somehow clasped around it.

That's how I came to be sitting on a bench in the middle of a sunny Texas afternoon. I could hear lots of people passing me, laughing and enjoying the mild temperature – a rarity for the end of spring. I allowed myself a moment to feel envious at their carefree chatter, knowing I had been the same less than a day before.

I sighed and opened my eyes, then looked down at my hand where the object sat immobile, utterly foreign and wrong. Some... being... had visited last night, in some form or other, and left me the scroll I'd so gingerly opened less than an hour before.

And I had no idea what to do with it.

I got up, unable to stay still and unwilling to keep reading. I needed help. And there was only one conspiracy theorist I knew who would believe me.

I pulled out my battered cell phone, scrolled through my contacts, and punched the number.

A familiar, lively voice quickly answered the ring, greeting me with warmth.

"Hey! It's been forever."

"I need to see you."

"Whoa. What's the problem?"

"Something only you can help me with."

His voice changed, immediately lowering and becoming quite serious.

"What're we talking about? Level 4 outbreak? Asteroids? Natural disaster?"

"No. Worse."

He paused, and I could practically see his brain whirling as it processed that short statement.

"Level 10, code red, end of the world, huh?"

I waited, letting my silence speak for me. I'd always ignored his crazy ideas and belief in all things weird, fantastic, and geeky. So he had to know something big had happened.

"Okay. Where are you? I'm on my way."

"No, not here. I'm at the San Pedro Springs Park. It's too... public. Do you have someplace secure, but not your house? Uh, you know, completely off the grid?"

"Yeah. Got it. I'll come pick you up and we'll head over there."

"Okay."

"Be there in twenty."

He hung up and I took a deep breath of air. The container hummed coldly against my skin.

And now I could feel it pulsing in sync with my heartbeat. The clock was ticking.

We keep a few survivors – to study, to dissect, to learn. We do this so that we can stay stronger than they. Sometimes they try to learn about us, try to communicate, to befriend us or ask for help, for mercy.

They can't comprehend they are what we used to be – weak.

Even more important is that they don't understand what they will become, as we once were: a remnant. Survivors of a world hanging on by gossamer streams of cosmic wind.

A horn honked, pulling me out of the words flickering behind my eyes. My head ached and my hand was starting to throb. The scroll dropped out of my hands.

"Okay, get in."

I opened the door, ignoring the scroll where it lay on the ground.

I knew it'd be back.

"Hello Fabian."

"Hello, Paulie."

I frowned at him, but he just laughed. Most of my friends just called me Lana, short for Paulana. But not Fabian. He'd always insisted on being different.

Fabian took off from the curb with a squeal.

"Where we going?"

"To my secret hideout."

I turned to him in surprise.

"You have a what?"

"A safe house, really, up by the lake, so about an hour away. It's completely protected from government hackers and satellite tracking. It's also got a state-of-the-art security system I designed."

"You never told me about this."

"It wouldn't be completely secure if I told anybody."

I looked over at his familiar floppy brown hair and thick glasses, his eyebrows creased in concentration and he drove.

"So why tell me now?"

He took a quick glance at me. His bright green eyes were, as always, startling.

"You said level 10, code red. This is what the house was built for. I can break the rules for that."

I smiled at him.

"Thank you."

We rode along a few more minutes until we hit the highway.

"Okay. Tell me."

So I told him everything that had happened since last night. He stayed quiet the entire time. It took longer than I expected, as I kept stopping to look down at my hands, waiting apprehensively for the alien scroll to reappear, hard and metallic, into my hand. Because inevitably as I wound down, he asked the question I'd been waiting for since I first called him.

"So where is this alien scroll?"

"I, uh, dropped it at the park."

He was silent for a few moments.

"We're almost there."

This surprised me, because I thought he'd laugh at my claims or at least insist on going back to retrieve the cylinder, but he did none of that. Instead, he turned his car onto a small track that led to the north side of the lake, which was, as far as I knew, uninhabited. We drove right up to a clump of brush that was completely impassable.

"Fabian?"

"It's okay, Paulie. Just wait."

He then shifted the car into park, jumped out, and strode straight towards the green wall. He reached his hand out, made some motion, and suddenly the entire middle section started moving, making an opening just large enough for his little car to get through.

He turned and walked back to the car.

"What? How did you... there's no way you could disguise a gate there. I can see right through that."

He smiled to himself as he put the car in gear.

"It's not a fence. That's too easy to track. Instead, I looped a series of counter weights in the shape of rocks and branches across that section. I then designed a sort of key made of interwoven silk – to look like a rather thick spider web – that activates the counter weights when I pull them in a certain pattern. It took me about a year to get it all together."

I was speechless as we drove through, for I could see no evidence that there was anything man-made about the gate.

After we passed the narrow opening, he repeated the procedure in reverse and the wall closed behind us. We then drove forward towards a tumble of rocks.

"Fabian – are you Batman?"

He laughed at me in his quiet way.

"No, Paulie. But this is pretty close to a bat cave."

He pulled the car up to the outmost rock and just before we ran into it, he swerved sharply left and wedged it under an outcropping.

"See, it's completely invisible from three sides."

"Wow. So, how do we get out?"

He slanted me a mischievous look.

"We climb."

So saying, he opened the sunroof and easily popped himself through the top. With a sense of surrealism, I unbuckled my seatbelt and followed him, though with a bit more struggle. He slid forward off the car towards a black recess in the rock. I followed suit.

"You ready?"

"Yeah."

He bent down and reached under the edge of the wall. His muscles contracted and suddenly the ground slid back to reveal a narrow hole. He fiddled at something then stood back.

"There you go."

It was a rope ladder, which he had unbound and let fall down.

"Are you kidding me?"

"You first, Paulie-girl."

I shot him a glare but he just chuckled, so I started down. It did not go down very far, so it only took a few minutes to reach the bottom. As my feet touched the ground, a dim light flickered on. I looked around in interest, but before I could do more than register a round room, Fabian dropped down beside me. I turned to ask him how he built this place, but as I opened my mouth, a familiar cold swept through my hands and I fell unconscious.

We broke our chains and we destroyed our oppressors. We embraced rage.

But when we returned to our home, we found broken bodies and spirits, broken ground and empty oceans. We swore to rebuild our planet.

No matter what and who we broke in turn.

Soft hands shook me, snapping me out of my faint.

"Paulie?"

I tried to open my eyes to reassure him, but the words I was reading didn't want to let me go, trying to push me down under again. I tried to raise my hands, but they were clutched tightly around the cold cylinder.

Then I understood. I gave in, and relaxed.

In that bare instant before surrendering, I whispered, "My hands."

Fabian immediately reached toward me and his warmth closed around the scroll.

However, though there is no remorse and compassion left in my DNA, still there is exhaustion. That was never erased. I am exhausted from spending all my life in pursuit of destruction. Haven't we traveled far enough? Eradicated enough species similar to our own, satisfied our aggression enough to finally return to our world, one which lives again. Aren't we safe enough?

What we once considered atrocities we have visited on hundreds of worlds. We have erased harmonious and advanced societies, many for whom war was naught but a myth. We have fought and annihilated because we now know nothing else.

We cannot understand our own histories.

Yet we deserve little mercy. Even now, through my exhaustion, I feel no remorse for the thousands I've killed. For the cries I've silenced. I cannot feel that which was taken from me without consent ages before I was conceived.

Still, there is a weight I carry behind these eyes that tells the tale of what I've seen and shows what paths I might have chosen.

Therefore, I write this now hoping that perhaps, if some world were told, were warned, they might prepare. Might be ready to fight us, to convince us that the cost is not worth the price. That our lives, as few as we are, are worth so much more. Perhaps then we might realize that we need to return home and destroy no others.

But I've not the power for that.

And so this message is for a journey of one... and it may not be enough.

We are coming. We will show no mercy. We will not stop. All within our sight will die. There is no defense, for you have not the technology to oppose us.

Save who you can, for you have no more time than the fleeting revolution of your planet around your sun to prepare.

I will do no more.

I woke up, the indigo lines fading from behind my eyes. I felt Fabian stirring next to me, his body also prone on the floor. His hands encircled mine, and I knew that he'd read the message with me, his touch somehow enabling him to see what I saw.

I turned my head to face him and read the sadness in his eyes. Tears came to mine as well and in an instant, we were holding each other.

The alien scroll was both a history and a warning.

"There's not much time, is there?"

"No."

"Should we tell the government?"

He was silent for a long time.

"Yes, but..."

"But we should also tell whoever we can."

I sat up and stared at the cylinder. It lay inert, finally warmed by the heat of my body. It was spent, its message given.

"Who will believe us?"

Fabian sat up next to me.

"Only those who choose to listen and believe."

I nodded slowly.

"We will become the remnant."

"What?"

"It was part of the earlier message. They were remnants of a time when their own world was nearly destroyed. He was telling us... not to do what they did. Because their people really are gone. What is left now is what destroyed them. In their effort to be strong, they forgot what they were. And now they truly are no more."

Fabian looked away. I grabbed his arm and forced his faced towards me.

"But we will be the remnant that remembers, that passes on, that stays true. Don't you understand? He, or whatever it was, was trying to give us an alternative to a new beginning. In his own way, he was trying to bring us hope."

We sat there in silence, feeling the absent presence of the alien in the space between us, wondering if we might face it someday. If it might try to kill us.

Or if we would kill it in return.

I was discovered returning to my ship, but it is of no import.

We are a proud race. We do not yield. We do not forgive. We do not fear. Therefore, I go now to my death, facing it proudly. I would rather end this way than participate in the newest genocide of yet another inferior species.

It is fitting that my own kind should destroy me for what they perceive to be cowardice, which is punishable by death according to our laws. Yet better they believe that than understand my true intent.

We are a lost people, eaten away by the bitterness of long eons spent roaming the frozen, hostile universe, one galaxy at a time, never stopping, never submitting, never loving.

Our race, in truth, died a long time ago.

We no longer fight to keep our planet alive; we fight because we know no other way.

This is why, despite my combat fatigue, the urge to destroy still burns within me - even as I understand how we have deceived ourselves.

Thus, I deny myself any true satisfaction of death in battle. Instead, I will simply close my eyes one final time. In this absolute way, I defy who I am, and honor who I should have been.

About SASFA

The San Antonio Sci-Fi & Fantasy Authors Association, or SASFA, began as an outgrowth of the SA Indie Book Fest. The founder and organizer, C.M. Bratton, discovered a community of local authors and wanted to meet more within the sci-fi & fantasy genres. Instead of organizing an all-encompassing event, C.M. envisioned a more mobile group of authors coming together to do joint events or share and inform each other about upcoming ones.
The goal is to promote reading indie sci-fi & fantasy authors located in the San Antonio, TX. area.
To keep up to date on author events, check out
www.facebook.com/sascififantasy
Or email sascififantasy@gmail.com

About the Authors

C.M. BRATTON is a multi-award-winning sci-fi and fantasy writer from San Antonio, TX. A member of the Texas Association of Authors, C.M. has published twenty books and a solo comic series. In addition, C.M. has been a writer for several film projects, including *Sanitarium* and *O.B.E. the graphic novel*. C.M. received her B.A.s in Theatre Arts & Spanish from Yale University, an M.A. in Drama from Texas Woman's University, and an M.F.A. in Creative Writing for Media Arts from Full Sail University (for which she was also the Valedictorian). Along with teaching undergraduate theatre and writing, C.M. is currently working on several writing projects. These include finishing the follow-up trilogy to the award-winning *Dragonlady Trilogy*, a sci-fi pilot for *Neon Gods*, and web series *Online Dating for Zombies* based on her award-winning zom-com series, *The R.Z.A. Chronicles*. From dragons to cyborgs to zombies (oh my!), C.M. looks forward to sharing more worlds with you.
For more information, check out www.cmbratton.com or www.facebook.com/writercmbratton
Twitter & Instagram: @writercmbratton

KEVIN LOONEY's first novel, *Echoes of the Forgotten*, was an Award-Winning Finalist in the fantasy category of the 2017 International Book Awards. Due in part to the influence of his siblings and grandfather, Kevin developed a love and respect for science fiction and fantasy at a young age. Watching recordings of Star Trek: The Next Generation during trips to his grandparents' house is still one of his fondest childhood memories. When not working or writing, Kevin can be found playing games or reading books with his son, binge watching television shows with his wife, or exploring other worlds and stories. Connect with Kevin on facebook.com/authorkevinlooney or twitter.com/kevinlooney05 or his oft-neglected, but still-loved blog: kevinlooneyblog.wordpress.com

PATRICK NEAL is a singer-songwriter/guitarist and indie author who strives to leave a bookmark in the literary world. He invites you inside the minds of his characters, lending a touch of real-life experience intertwined with fiction. To see the list of books he has published to date, visit his author website at:
pattybug76.wixsite.com/patrick-neal

JT STREET is an EMMY-nominated storyteller and life-long lover of tales, be they true, fantastic, or both. When he's not plotting pitfalls for his protagonists, he enjoys tracking down stories and helping people share them with the world. He also loves spending time with his family and reading to his young daughter (and yes, he does ALL the funny voices). Learn more about his story at
www.soflymarketing.com/jt-street/

MICHAEL WIGINGTON Unbeknownst to many, Michael, a native Texan, is an immortal who sat at the Round Table with King Arthur & listened to the wisdom of Merlin. His father, when Michael asked if he could help a halfling take a ring to Mordor, told him to go mow the yard instead. Thankfully, he was allowed to go with Jason after the Golden Fleece & fight against a horde of skeleton warriors. When he was 16, he was tied to the mast of a ship with Ulysses and heard the sirens sing. He traveled to France with the Scarlet Pimpernel & helped him free nobles. Some fun facts: Michael lost his pet dragon, "Old Blue," in a Gwent game against Zotlan the dwarf. After spending ten years in Azeroth, he decided it was time to move back to Texas. These days he spends his time between Texas and the Corvarix Age kingdoms. Michael writes the tales of those lands until his lovely wife, Kara, says it's time for dinner. Find him at: www.fantasyinmyveins.com
https://twitter.com/MikeWig68
https://www.facebook.com/michaelwigingtonauthor/
Instagram @m_wigington_author

About the Artist

ROBOT 9000 aka LUIS A. RUIZ is a graduate of Savannah College of Art and Design, with a BFA in Computer Animation. He's currently a Senior Instructor at the Art Institute San Antonio and Otis College of Art and Design. Luis is self-taught, with over 22 softwares under his belt that include Adobe CC Suite, Autodesk Maya/Mudbox/Max, McNeel Rhino, Dassault Solid Works, Avid ProTools, Ableton Live, Chaos Group V-Ray, etc. Luis has worked in many industries that include TV, Film, Toy Design, and now Education. A short list of some of his clients include Disney, Mattel, Honda, Nintendo USA, Yahoo, Harley Davidson, Direct TV, & Thompson Reuters. Luis is a serious Renaissance artist that is continually learning new skills and softwares to create and teach amazing works in the field of artistic multimedia. Namaste.
Find him at: robot9000@gmail.com
Instagram @robot9000

And don't forget to check out
SASFA's award-winning book,

Secondary Worlds
Sci-Fi & Fantasy Poetry

Order copies at Amazon.com
or message us at
www.facebook.com/sascififantasy

www.ingramcontent.com/pod-product-compliance
Lightning Source LLC
LaVergne TN
LVHW010248100625
813479LV00018B/340